ALICE
AGAIN

Adrienne Leslie

Published by
Flynn and Park Street Press
New London, New Hampshire 033257
www.flynnandparkstreetpress.com

Book Design by Linda Tyler
Book Cover by Hyun Soo Na

Copyright © 2014 Adrienne Leslie

Additional Transliterations by Hyun Joo (H J) Lee
Flynn and Park Street Press
All rights reserved.

Printed and bound in the United States of America.
10 9 8 7 6 5 4 3 2

PUBLISHER'S CATALOGING-IN-PUBLICATION

Leslie, Adrienne
Alice Again/ Adrienne Leslie
ISBN 978-0-9903233-0-3
ISBN 978-0-9903233-1-0
1.   Leslie, Adrienne. 2. Fiction—Fantasy—Romance
Library of Congress Control Number: 2014941863
Published by Flynn and Park Street Press

Visit www.amazon.com to order additional copies.

ACKNOWLEDGEMENTS

I take this space to note it was by accident that my character, Hoon shared his last name with a 9/11 victim, but it was my choice to keep her name, Gye Hyong Park, in this story to honor her memory.

Alice Again would have remained a wisp of an idea without the steadfast encouragement from Joni Cole and Deb Franzoni of The White River Junction Writers' Workshop. I send special thanks for the inspiration from my fellow board members at The Korean-American Scholarship Foundation; especially my friend, Peter Boklim Choi, author of The Mountain Rats. Thanks too for information on all things biblical (which means all things) from Pastor Stephen Ro of Living Faith Community Church and Peter Ong of Kings Cross Church. I am indebted to the multi-talents of Hyun-Soo Na, the *wakie-mad* brilliance of Linda Tyler, the wisdom of Hala Faid and most grateful for the spiritual backing and wanton frivolity of The Kakao Women. I remain in awe of the tech-help from my son, the love of my family and the endless sustenance from sister of my heart, Lyn. Not least is my sincere gratitude for Queensborough Community College adjunct instructor Margaret McConnell as well as The Sunday Readers, including; Hannah Kang, Sabrina Ng and Jordan Sung. And for Him who provided three side-by-side windows in a little house that let in the light of a thousand red sky sunrises, I am amazed by your grace.

This book is dedicated to Madeleine Josephine
my *Palan Nun Aghesshi*

Chapter

1: If Wishes Were Horses

There's something better out there—Travel Rapid Eastern Metro! I re-read the bus company's ad on the back of the menu twice to keep my mind off the bread basket. It didn't help. I plucked out a salt-crusted bread stick and slathered it in butter.

Why should I count carbs on my birthday?

On four evenings each year we, the members of Carlucci's Ristorante's Birthday Dinner Club, would meet to celebrate. That sultry summer Friday of 2009, was my night. Carlucci's drew a crowd whatever the season, not for its cuisine or ambiance but for its ample parking lot, a valuable asset in car-loving Queens, New York.

Laura, Ilene and I were seated at our usual table beneath the sooty ceiling fan when Peg, silvery wisps of hair clinging to the sweat on her forehead, rushed in late. She was an adjunct professor at Adelphi University and at sixty-four, two years older than us. She was also the only one with a full time job.

"Have you ordered your salads yet or am I the only thing at this table that's wilted?" she quipped. Over the years, Peg's sense of humor had soothed my soul. If she hadn't had a teaching career while I was home raising twin boys, I'm sure we would have been best friends.

"Sit down and cool off. I was just talking about that thief, Dr. Gold." Laura pointed to the lone empty chair for our friend.

"Which Dr. Gold are you calling a thief, Lau?" Peg lifted the bread basket by its handles. "The one in Great Neck across from the Thai restaurant or the one near TJ Maxx?"

"The TJ Maxx's Gold is my dentist. I'm talking about my dermatologist." Laura tucked a lock of faux-auburn hair behind her ear and pointed to her cheek. "He wanted to charge me twelve hundred dollars for Cosmelan injections even though he couldn't guarantee they would fade my age spots."

We stopped eating our salads to inspect Laura's spots. Divorced and alone, she obsessed over every new sign of aging. There wasn't a cream or laser treatment she hadn't tried and we knew she would have sold her soul for the price of a facelift. Yet, for as long as I had known her, she had put off surgery to correct her lazy eye. "I'm not so vain that I'd go under the knife for my strabismus," she'd tell me even though I never asked. I had heard her strabismus defense regularly and it always left me wondering why she'd choose something to make her look better rather than see better.

Laura and I had been friends since she moved next door when our children were toddlers. Too often I found her snarky and sometimes downright mean, yet I car pooled and hit local tag sales with her. Although Peg may have been a better choice as confidante, I, like Carlucci's customers, had chosen convenience over sustenance.

The four of us sat behind our salads with thick ranch dressing in mini plastic cups on the side. Salad dressing served this way is supposed to aid portion control but as we talked, we drowned our greens in the cups. Then we all asked for seconds on the dressing.

"I had two doctors with the same last name." Peg began. "That's a mistake I won't make again. One was Dr. Carl Lee, gynecologist. The other was George Lee, my foot doctor. Once, I thought I called the *gyno* about my hormone replacement therapy. I wanted to check out my side effects so I phoned him from the car to make sure he was in."

Peg stopped to snatch a garlic knot. "You know, I can't drive with my readers and I can't read without them so I couldn't make out which number was C. Lee and which was G. Lee. Anyway, I got the receptionist. She says, 'Dr. Lee's office.' I tell her I'm Peg Tolan, his patient, and that the menopause meds he put me on really made me sick. My belly was popping out, my breasts were hot and I was very wet…down there. I'm waiting for an answer so long; I thought the phone went dead. Then she said, 'You've reached Dr. Lee the podiatrist.'"

"What did you say?" I asked.

"I said, 'Oh well, never mind, this is *Meg Bolan* hanging up now!'"

"Quick thinking." I wished I could tell a story like Peg.

"Hmph," Laura snorted as she doused a cucumber with dressing. "I doubt that your name change did anything at all." We could always count on Laura to put Peg down though I was never sure why.

Ilene stopped checking her cell messages to laugh out loud at Peg's punch line. "I have to tell my daughter-in-law that story," she said. Then she flipped the cell phone closed to rifle through the bread basket. "Aren't there any more onion rolls? I'm still starving. All I had to eat today was Caulder's burnt Eggos this morning." Caulder was Ilene's granddaughter and her preferred topic of conversation. Ilene triumphantly lifted the last roll. "Caulder was crying and kicking while I tried to figure out how the exhaust fan under the micro works. I was afraid the toaster would trigger my son's house alarm again. The last time that happened, we had half the Larchmont fire department show up."

"You ate burnt Eggos?" I asked, wondering if I would have liked babysitting my grandchildren every day.

"By the time I hit the right button, the stupid thing was charred. I couldn't feed it to a two-year old. But I couldn't just throw it out," Ilene explained.

How many dinners had we eaten together? I tallied up the years. We originally met as young mothers at the Glen Oaks Playground. As our children grew up and moved on, we morphed into a birthday dinner club. I had planned to defect from the group in 2001 after Peg convinced me to apply to graduate school for creative writing. But before I could, the twin towers of the World Trade Center exploded into rubble, killing 2,753 souls including police officer Luke Pleasance, my first born. I added my future to everything else that died that day. And yet another birthday passed as if I was still alive inside, I took comfort in my glass of rosé. If I can't be happy, I can at least be numb.

Laura slipped off her cardigan to reveal her well-tanned arms. "Look at my chin," she pointed at her jawline. Laura's conversation always moved from injectables to cosmetic surgery at our birthday gatherings. "When I pull up right here below my earlobe, see how great I look. Try it," she commanded.

My tablemates pushed up on their cheeks till the loose skin reached their brows.

"Come on you too, Alice," Laura insisted. "Now that you're 62, it's time to break out the Juvederm!"

"Alice looks great," Peg said as she patted my back. "She's absolutely the hottest woman who ever collected Social Security. Just ask Mike."

"He's probably warming up the bed sheets right now," I said a bit too loudly and looked down at my hands to hide my embarrassment. That morning, I had treated myself to a manicure. Petal Pink. But why did I bother? I couldn't remember the last time Mike and I held hands. Mike and I have spent the last eight years living like polite roommates. Not even roommates because most nights he sleeps in the den.

"Laura, when are you going to start dating again?" Ilene pressed.

"It's Alice's birthday. We should focus on her," Laura said as she held her wine glass up to the light. "Look how smudged this is. I should call the waiter over."

We let Laura divert our attention away from her love life. Who could blame her? Her ex-husband had dumped her and taken away the step-daughter she had raised for twelve years. When they divorced, Laura lost her whole family. A new man was probably the last thing on her mind.

Four plates of broiled salmon with double orders of string beans were dealt to us like playing cards. "Alice, do you have extra cucumbers in your garden?" Ilene asked cutting into her fish. "Caulder loved them. It's the only vegetable she'll eat without coaxing."

The conversation had turned as predictable as the meal. Eventually, a chocolate frosted monolith was brought to our table by a new server—a young, dark-eyed man in tight black jeans. He topped the cake with two candles, a pink 6 and a white 2. He reminded me of my first high school crush—tall, thin and a great kisser. Too bad he moved away in our senior year.

My cheeks heated up. Why is this birthday bringing out the what-might-have-been in me?

Laura switched the order of the candles so they read twenty-six. "Voila!" she proclaimed. I hadn't seen her so animated in years. Maybe she was dating.

"See how easy it is to be young again?" she said as she elbowed my side.

"I'd settle for fifty-two," I reminisced over the candlelight.

"I'd even do sixty-two again," Peg added, and tucked her gift for me between our chairs. "It's a silk nightie. You and Mike can celebrate later."

Ilene took Peg's cue and reached around my cake to hand me a day-spa gift certificate. "Many more, Alice," she said. "In good health." She blew a kiss across our table.

Laura rapped on her new wineglass for attention then placed an emerald silk tote with an elaborate top-knot next to my cake. "This is from that little herb shop on Northern. The owner's a Korean guy named Mr. Kim. Everybody at work swears by his medicinal seeds."

I loosened the tie to remove a small sachet that looked like the little plastic packets found in new coat pockets, the ones that absorb the damp so we won't know they come from overseas sweat shops.

"Mr. Kim is famous for his sleep aids," Laura went on. "You should start tonight."

I tore off a corner and sniffed. The seeds smelled organic, not exactly pungent, but earthy like rain-soaked soil. I sprinkled a few into my palm. They were ruby red and as tiny as strawberry seeds. "Are they eaten or steeped like tea?" I asked.

Ilene put on her readers to scrutinize the business card among the sachets. "Shouldn't you ask your doctor if it's OK to take Oriental medicine?"

"At our age, we've got to be careful with drug interactions," Peg agreed.

Our waiter returned with three cups of coffee and Laura's tea.

I wondered what young women talked about. I thought of Luke's girlfriend, Emma, a California transplant with a ready smile and a devotion to jogging. We should have tried to get to know each other better. I suppose we thought we had a lifetime to do that. Emma moved back to Carmel a few years ago. I hoped she had found another good man.

"Alice, you're supposed to swallow them. Take them tonight so you'll finally get a good night's sleep," Laura urged as she jammed Mr. Kim's card into my purse. "Keep this for refills."

What the heck. I had already tried every cure from alcohol to Ambien for my chronic insomnia. Why not try seeds?

"Happy birthday to you, happy birthday dear Alice," Laura began singing. I clapped along. Even the wait-staff joined in. *Maybe the back end of this year will be better.*

"Make a wish!"

"What are you going to wish for?"

I knew I'd be the turd in the punchbowl if I said my real wish aloud. "I'll just say a little prayer in silence, OK?" I closed my eyes. *Please, Lord turn back time to September 10th, 2001. I want to be Alice Pleasance, mother of twin sons with their whole lives ahead of them, not the Pieta I've become.*

I blew. The flames flickered then righted themselves.

"Very funny, who bought the trick candles?" Laura stink-eyed Ilene.

"They're regular candles," Ilene defended herself. "Try again, Alice."

"And say your wish out loud," Peg added. "You're among friends."

"Here's my wish. I wish…I just wish…."

"Come on, Alice," Laura coaxed.

"I swear, Alice, these aren't trick candles." Ilene pointed to their waxy puddles as proof.

The waiter placed a milk pitcher and sugar bowl in front of me. His cologne was musky like a scent that was popular years ago. "I wish…that one more time in my life a young, dark-eyed man in tight jeans would notice me," I blurted out.

Then in one breath, I snuffed out the candles.

Chapter

2: Her Lamp Burns Late Into the Night

Laura and I drove home together as we had done after every Carlucci dinner.

"I didn't want to point it out in front of the others." Laura began, "but you've looked so tired lately."

I didn't answer. Laura could be really callous. It's a wonder she didn't add that I'd put on a few pounds too.

"Really, Alice," Laura insisted, "take the seeds as soon as you get in. You'll drift right off. Mike's probably sleeping anyway."

"No, he's waiting up to give me my birthday gift. I'll surprise him with my new nightie from Peg," I said. What if he really is? And what would he do if I did?

The houses in Floral Park, Queens are far from palatial. I pulled into the narrow driveway that separated my lawn from Laura's. "I'll wait for you to go in," I assured her. "There were two burglaries in Glen Oaks last week."

"I'll be fine," Laura muttered as she got out. It was clear her party mood was over, but I had long stopped wondering what triggered her irritability.

I walked up my drive. The kitchen nightlight just beyond the blinds sent prickly blue shafts through the window. Next to it, the living room drapes were drawn, making my home look more like a one-eyed haunted house than a sanctuary.

I was delighted to find Mike sitting up in our bed reading. I took in his high English forehead and salt and pepper hair. He had the same birthday as Mick Jagger and under the reading lamp he looked like a cool, albeit chunky, version of an aging rock star.

"Did you have fun with the girls?" he asked.

I held up my new nightie. "Want to have fun now?" I regretted the come-on as soon as I spoke.

He took two Tums from a roll on his night stand. "You should have told me before you left," he said. "I had a leftover pork chop before I came to bed."

Tonight's excuse was indigestion. The last time I asked, it was fatigue. With all the hype about middle-aged men and Viagra, my husband was more comfortable saying "no thanks" than visiting his urologist.

The house phone rang as if to save me further embarrassment. I chucked my birthday gifts onto the bureau and grabbed the receiver.

My son William, born seven minutes after Luke, had an even lovelier face than his brother. When they were little, I strutted when I visited the playground with my heir and the spare. They were a beautiful set of twins and except for one night of coitus, I took all the credit.

"Hello, my darling boy, what's up?"

"I am calling to say happy birthday. I texted you on your new Android. Did you see it?" he asked.

Will had helped me buy a cell phone a few days earlier but I still didn't know how it worked. "I'm charging it now. Can't wait to start texting," I lied.

"Mom, you know who I was with today? Ruthie Cole. You remember her, right? She went to Higher and Higher Academy with me, but then she moved away. Her family is visiting in New York. Do you know where they live, Mom? In Africa!" he said, his voice shaking with excitement. No one hearing him would guess he had recently turned thirty-five. "Ruthie saw elephants and touched them. Elephants in Africa have bigger ears than Asian elephants. The phant in elephant means huge which, when you think about it, makes sense."

When Will was ten months old, he still couldn't roll over, didn't follow my finger or grab for shiny toys like Luke did. By the end of their second year, I had taken Will to five pediatricians. Each doctor visit began with tests and ended with a physician saying, "I'm sorry." When he turned six, Will was finally diagnosed with Asperger's syndrome. Will's IQ was average, but his challenges were not. Five years after Luke's death, Will moved into the Ladders Facility for high functioning autistic adults.

I loved hearing the happy energy in his voice, but his counselors said to work on his social skills by keeping him on topic.

"Yes, I remember Ruthie. Her parents are missionaries," I said gently as I rerouted our conversation. "I'm glad you called. I'm wearing the cross you bought me. I put it on this morning and I'll never take it off."

"Come on, Mom. Never?"

"Never. Did you want to talk to Dad?"

"No. I have to feed Peter and Paul."

"All right, darling." I blew three kisses before hanging up.

"Didn't Will want to talk to me?" Mike asked.

"No. He was rushing off to feed his fish."

Mike was hurt. I could see it in his face. But Mike's way of coping without Luke was to force Will to be more like his brother. I knew he would have pumped Will for the Mets' starting lineup instead of asking about his fish. I hated being the buffer between my husband and son.

I slipped into the bathroom and faced the mirror. My lipstick had worn off at dinner, leaving only the waxy plum liner. On my fair skin, it made me look like a vampire. I needed to moisturize. The department store wrinkle cream I'd bought cost a fortune and reeked like an old whore. Where was the sweet-faced girl I used to be? I pushed up on my greased skin till my fingertips reached my temples. My jawline tightened and the apples of my cheeks reappeared. There she is, not gone after all. Just a little deeper inside me.

Mike was snoring by the time I returned to the bedroom. How he could drop off in less than a minute was quite beyond me. I refolded the new nightie leaving the tags in place, and reached under my pillow for my pajamas.

I had just drifted off when my arrhythmia shook me awake. Night after night, I awakened with an unruly heartbeat that left me lightheaded and anxious. Dr. Camden had assured me that this was simply a symptom of "the changes." He suggested I splash my face with cold water whenever my heart pounded and wrote a prescription for pills that only masked its intensity.

I patted down the sheets to locate the television remote and surfed till landing on an Asian love story. A pretty girl with soulful eyes walked away from an equally pretty boy. *"Kah ji mah,"* he called after her. I read the sub-titles at the bottom of the screen: "Don't leave." I wondered if she'd really go. When Mike and I had been married about three years, I knew we were wrong for each other. I'd thought about leaving, but there was always a reason not to. I didn't want to upset my parents, I was afraid the boys would suffer, and after 9/11....

Too much thinking for one night. I grabbed the silk bag off the bureau and found the opened packet.

The seeds were sweet and crunchy like sesame candy. I swallowed them with bathroom tap water and got back into bed. I didn't bother shutting off my lamp. In an hour or two, I'd probably need the light to find the remote again.

Chapter

3: Beautiful Dreamer

I pried open one eye to read the cable box—11:30 p.m.

As I suspected, Korean seeds were no match for American insomnia. Although I had to admit, with just an hour's sleep, I felt rested and without the usual urge to pee, but went anyway.

I kept the bathroom light off as I sat on the bowl, leaning my elbows on my thighs. My legs felt different. Hard. Tight. Were my thighs getting stiff? I just turned sixty-two, not eighty-two. Why would I begin to atrophy?

After wiping and pulling up my pajama bottoms, a sudden surge of vertigo nearly felled me. I grabbed the sink for support.

What was in those seeds?

My arrhythmia thumped my insides. I slapped cold tap water on my cheeks and shook with chills. I wiped the drops from my face and blinked back at a watery apparition in my bathroom mirror.

Her blonde hair spilled to her shoulders in waves. She became startled and placed her hand over her mouth. I felt my lips. She touched hers too. I ran my fingers through my hair. So did she. Why was I looking at a younger version of me in the mirror? I'm hallucinating! What did those seeds do to my brain?

I flicked on the bathroom light. My own hand on the switch was smooth and plump. My nails were longer. I looked down at my legs. No spider veins, no misplaced freckles. Except for the scar on my knee from when I was seven and fell at the skating rink, my gams were perfect. I checked out my lady bits under my pajamas. *Whoa!* I took the bathroom scale from its hiding place next to the bowl and put it flat on the tiles. My new beautiful feet pressed on the platform as I hoped I weighed as good as I looked.

Holy cow, 119.4!

I couldn't help myself, I pulled off my PJ's and jumped naked onto the scale. I was a miraculous 118. Down twenty-six pounds. Even after Carlucci's chocolate cake. This is the best dream ever. I'm never waking up, never, never, never.

The face in the mirror shared my elation.

But how could a dream turn back the years? And, if it did, does that mean everything has gone back? How many Sundays in church had I begged God to let me see Luke again? Is this His answer? Is Luke still alive?

Within seconds, I was downstairs in the boys' bedroom.

When Will moved to Ladders, I left the space as it was. I'd meant to make it into a study. But since I didn't, it became what I hoped it wouldn't be—a shrine for Luke.

The room held only the twin maple dressers and mirrors. It was the same as it was the last time I vacuumed and dusted. The beige walls were yellowed and the plaid rug should have been donated to the church bazaar years ago. I had longed to see the bunk beds or the shelves filled with Gundam robots and Mets' souvenirs but the corner that housed baseball bats and skateboards was, like the rest of their room, empty.

In their closet, Luke's tuxedo still hung at the very end of the rack faithfully waiting to be worn again.

September ninth, two days before he died, Luke and Emma were in a wedding party. They stopped by after the reception for Will to see his brother in a tuxedo.

"OK, Bro? You've seen me duded up," Luke said as he posed for his brother's camera before changing into jeans and a tee. "It feels good to be out of that monkey suit," he joked before tossing his dress clothes onto Will's bed.

How blasé we were over our joy that Sunday. I had busied myself in the kitchen with plates and cups instead of drinking in the last normal conversation we'd share. I flattered Emma's slender shape while silently wondering when they'd get married and give me a grandchild. I remember being tired and grateful they weren't stopping long. Luke headed for Will's room to fetch his evening clothes. To hurry Luke off, I offered to take them to the dry cleaners later that week. On Tuesday, terrorists murdered my son.

I pulled the lapels towards me to breathe in the wool that rested on the back of his neck. Even though his essence had faded, I took solace in touching the jacket that survived him. I put my hands into his sleeves, swinging them to and fro. For one pretend moment, I was holding the hands of baby Luke, sharing our bedtime nursery rhyme.

Starlight, star bright, first star I see tonight. Wish I may, wish I might have the wish I wish tonight.

I patted the buttons and straightened the pocket handkerchief.

Oh, Luke, why didn't I dream you were young again instead of me? The single bulb left in the ceiling fixture flickered as the closet door squeaked to a close. Maybe I'm not young, just younger. Luke could still be alive, but not here. He'll be home in Bayside with Emma!

I tiptoed up to my bedroom to get my clothes, making a point of not looking in Mike's direction. If Mike was the same as I left him, then Luke was dead. Right now, I had to believe we were all pre 9/11.

I can be at Luke's in fifteen minutes. Maybe Emma will put up coffee. In the morning, Luke can make a bakery run and we'll feast on bagels with mountains of cream cheese topped with English marmalade. It'll be a dream come true.

I dressed in the boys' room. My chinos slid down to my hips. Thankfully, no woman ever throws away her favorite jeans. I rummaged through the dressers' drawers till I resurrected an old tank top and a size 5 pair of bell-bottoms. I zipped up commando style, grabbed my keys, and slipped out the kitchen door.

Chapter

4: Revelation

Whirling mist the color of spring violets curled around my arms and shoulders as I stepped outside. I double-tapped my car's key and its headlights blinked twice, illuminating the dewdrops on the grass till they sparkled like amethysts.

I sped down the driveway in reverse then headed west. The wipers kept time on the dampened windshield till the first traffic light—soon, soon, soon, soon—when the fog lifted like a stage curtain.

무궁화

My son's street was as I remembered it, a mishmash of condos and attached houses too close to the Bayside railroad station and noisy nightlife of Bell Boulevard. The only change on the street was a massive sign with a pulsating neon rooster at the corner— *Wakie says: This zone is in First Watch! Midnight to Noon Time Now— 12:31 a.m. Have a great Watch!*

I pounded on Luke's door. I have to convince him the towers will fall. He and Emma must stay at our house with Mike and Will. We all have to be together.

A chubby young woman with soft brown eyes opened Luke's door only as far as the security chain would allow. The lamp light behind her haloed her head. "Is something wrong? Are you all right, Miss?" she asked.

Was I at the wrong house? I stepped back to look at the number. 214-12. It was the right address. But weren't the numbers on the other side of the doorway the last time I was here?

"I'm looking for Luke. Luke and Emma?"

"You must have the wrong address. The house numbers repeat on each street. What street were you looking for?" she asked.

"I'm on the right street. Forty-Third Avenue. This is my son's house," I snapped.

"Did someone give you this address?" She looked at me as if I was crazy. "Maybe your son's father?"

"My son and his girlfriend bought this house, not my husband." I suddenly realized I'd shown up in the middle of the night in this young body declaring I had a son my own age.

The woman's smile flattened. "Would you like me to call someone?"

The silhouette of a man emerged behind her. "Maria, where's my shirt?" he asked. She answered him in another language. It was just a few words but I guessed they probably translated into, "Honey, call the police."

How far back in time had I gone? Maybe, it was the wrong year. Maybe Luke and Emma haven't moved here yet. I mustn't sound insane but I need to hear it's before September 11th, 2001.

"I'm sorry I woke you," I said in my calmest voice as I struggled to think of a logical reason for my appearance. "Obviously, I'm mistaken. I must have had a little too much to drink on the Boulevard."

"That's all right. I rise early First Watch to read my Bible." Her smile returned. "Can you get home by yourself? What's your name, Miss?"

She waited for my answer.

"I'm Alice...." I stopped. It would be better not to give my last name.

There we stood, young me on the front step and smiling Maria behind the security chain. The links slackened as the space between door and jamb narrowed. "I will pray for you, Alice," she offered. "Wait." I had to get her to say it. "Just one more thing and I'll go. Please. Tell me today's date. All of it, including the year."

She fixed her gaze on the sign behind me. *Wakie says: This zone is in First Watch! Midnight to Noontime   Time Now—12:37 a.m. Have a great Watch!* Underneath the bright-eyed rooster in police cap and whistle, a zipper message sped along: *August 16, 2009. Mets vs. SF Giants Citi Field 1:10 p.m. Second Watch.*

Chapter

5: Once in a Blue Moon

It would have been suicidal to drive in the state I was in. I walked past my car and down to the street corner.

Bell Boulevard was feverish with late night revelers. Crowded bars and restaurants side by side and facing each other ran from Bayside Village down to the bay. I began running, weaving among strangers until I stopped to catch my breath. The Blue Moon Pub door swung out, releasing a young couple dressed in identical striped shirts who shared a kiss and a cigarette. The opened doorway sent a plume of scotch and tobacco smoke into the night air. For a moment, I wondered how they got away with smoking in there.

Because this is just a dream, I told myself, like driving to Luke's house and meeting a stranger under his porch lamp. I'm just stumbling through scenes from a seed-induced hallucination.

I took in a deep cleansing breath and let it out slowly to calm down.

Inside, a lively crowd pressed against the tinted glass window. I could use a shot of something to settle my nerves, I thought. I guess a fantasy cocktail will have to do. I slipped into the bar unnoticed.

I felt the steady drumbeat of an unfamiliar song. The Blue Moon's tables and bar were stainless steel that shimmered under the lights. A young man in a pink golf shirt and pastel madras shorts standing near the door tried to light his cigarette. "I think these matches are dead," he said, holding the book in my direction. "What do you think?"

His golden tan and sun-streaked hair perfected his summer ensemble; a style called The Full Hampton back in my flower child days.

He gave me the once over. "We just got into New York. Been sailing. You sail?" he asked.

At the end of each phrase, he tried to light his smoke with a wilted match. For a motherly moment, I was about to enumerate the perils of smoking. Instead, I handed him a fresh matchbox from the bar. After all, what could happen to this figment of my imagination? He'd get make-believe emphysema?

His teal eyes watered as he drew in the nicotine. "You're very nice. I'm gonna buy you a drink. I'm John. What's your name?"

Even in a crumpled golf shirt, he was cute. Why not enjoy a pretend drink with the first man to offer to pay for me since the end of the Vietnam War.

John introduced me to his crew—three other bronzed yachtsmen who sailed from Dennis Port, Massachusetts to Bayside Marina and drank till morning.

He ordered me an apple-tini. As soon I finished it, he ordered another. I nursed the second. Two were my limit.

"They should name these after you, cuz you're the apple of my eye," he tapped his glass on mine.

Do young men still use cheesy pick-up lines? I soon forgot my limit and polished off a third cocktail. Eventually, the tinis took their toll on me and my eye-lids grew heavy.

"Alice, let's get some fresh air," John tugged my arm.

Outside, the street traffic still hummed. We walked a few steps down the boulevard. "I've been wanting to taste your lips all Watch." John leaned me up against a shop window. Is this guy kissing me? Married me? Have I just broken my vows for a total stranger in plaid shorts?

He used his tongue like a screwdriver to pry open my mouth. Not happening. Not even in a three-cocktail dream. I pinched his skinny waist.

"New York girls usually say yes," he said, rubbing his side with his palm.

New York girls? Is he trying to be funny? "You mean all four million of us?" I shot back.

John flashed a winsome smile. "OK, Alice. Don't worry. I don't go where I'm not welcomed and I sure as hell don't come where I'm not welcomed. I'm going back inside. One more for the road? I'm buying."

Above the street lights, I glimpsed a patch of sky.

"I should head home," I begged off. "It'll be dawn soon. The sky's already red."

"It's still night-red. Sun-up is hours away." He took his phone from his pocket to show me the screen. "Look. It's only three— First Watch."

I nodded as if I understood. "Thanks for the cocktails. It was very gracious of you, but I'm going to call it a night."

"Alice, you're the most polite girl who ever turned me down," John said. He kissed my cheek, opened the Blue Moon door and was gone.

I wondered if that cute young man with his brusque embrace really existed. There's one thing I knew for sure. Even in his wildest dreams he wouldn't have believed who he really kissed.

I took out my car keys and made a moving shadow under the bloodshot sky.

Chapter

6: Morning Has Broken

Mike stood at the foot of our bed holding my coffee mug, his meaty finger squeezed through its handle.

"I'm sorry I fell asleep on your birthday," he apologized. "Coffee?"

I took the mug and looked at my hands—short nails in Petal Pink polish. Of course it was a dream, I told myself. Besides, Mike isn't screaming "Who are you and what have you done with my wife?" I look exactly as he expects me to.

"Do you want bagels, Alice? I can pick some up." The half-closed vertical window blinds let in enough morning light to stripe Mike's face like prison bars.

"Please get me my headache pill," I moaned. My temples throbbed. I sure felt my age.

"There." He pointed to a Fioricet on my night stand. "Did you have a rough night?"

"Rough doesn't begin to describe it." Memories of the night before flashed like flip-book pages. I went to Bayside to find Luke. Somehow I ended up in a bar where a twenty-something yachtsman with a golden tan bought me drinks and later kissed me. Had I really been young and tempting enough for a stranger's sidewalk smooch?

"If you can't sleep, Alice, don't roam the floors all night, just take something," Mike insisted.

"Was I roaming last night?"

"Couldn't say. You know me, I'll sleep through anything." He headed for the door.

Had I been sleep-walking? Sleep kissing? I ran my tongue over my parched lips. Still as kisses go, last night's wasn't that bad.

무궁화

I looked full into my bathroom mirror. The corner of my mouth felt tender at the spot where John kept poking his tongue. But that was impossible because there was no John. I probably bit myself while I was dreaming. What was in those seeds that had me chewing my cud like a farm animal in my sleep? I showered to wash the dream away.

A clatter of dishes fan-fared my entry to the kitchen. Mike had shoved his dirty breakfast plates to the middle of the table, and was mindlessly adding another shot of half-and-half to his coffee. Why did I bother buying the skim milk his doctor recommended? I poured myself a cup of coffee and topped off his too. He grunted his thanks.

As soon as Mike went upstairs to watch the local news, I lifted my arms up over my head then bent down to touch my toes. No nerve jabs, no sore bunion. Even my headache was gone. Maybe the seeds were beneficial after all.

I took a box of cereal from the cabinet. But what if they had long term side-affects? Could one dose damage my brain?

Just outside the window, a fat robin swooped down and landed on the flower box. His belly was the color of last night's sky. I'd never dreamed so vividly before. Still, my fantasies belonged in my imagination not pumping through my bloodstream. But what if those things really happened? That's crazy. If it was real, I should have kept searching for Luke.

I felt an all too common tightening in my chest. Why had I taken those stupid seeds?

무궁화

The dog days of August made dressing a chore. I settled on a thin cotton top and the chinos that swam on me the night before. If I hurried, I could exchange Peg's nightie at Macy's and return Laura's gift to the herb shop before the heat of the day. I retrieved the remaining packets of seeds from my bureau and slipped on my sandals. Where had I left my handbag?

Since the day we moved in, the shelf at the kitchen door had been the repository of our outside lives, the resting place of purses, wallets and car keys. The boys, when young, found it convenient temporary storage for baseball mitts and soccer cleats.

That morning the shelf was bare. Was the handbag on my nightstand?

"Mike, did I leave my purse upstairs?" I shouted from the bottom of the stairway.

"No. There's nothing here." He came down in a fresh golf shirt and khakis.

"Are you leaving?" I asked.

He stopped at the hallway mirror, licked his fingertips and plucked a wiry gray hair from the top of his head. "While you were in the shower, Auntie called again," he griped.

Auntie was Mike's aunt Victoria, named after the queen. At ninety, her dementia haphazardly gnawed at her past, her childhood memories succumbing as easily as her memories of what she ate for lunch. It didn't, however, stop her demanding nature.

"What did she want?" I checked the dining room for my bag.

"The old girl can't find her lower dentures. She wants me to move her credenza away from the wall to take a look. I'll be back by lunchtime," he promised.

As usual, a call from Auntie meant an errand for Mike. This must be the third time this week.

"Why couldn't her home health aide find her teeth?" I asked.

"Beats me." Mike opened the hall closet. "Did you look in here?"

"Of course I looked there," I muttered to myself wondering if most unhappy couples stayed married just to have help finding their stuff.

I was sure I tossed my bag on the bureau after I came back from dinner. Why wasn't it there? I replayed the evening. I dreamed I woke up and drove to Luke's house. I drank in a bar, kissed a stranger and drove back. When I came home, I scooped up my pajamas off the boys' rug. Had I left my bag in the boys' room?

My jeans and tee shirt from the night before were heaped on the twins' carpet with my purse propping up the pile. Had I really left the house and come back late? I remembered being tired and tipsy enough to sashay naked to the bathroom. Had Mike seen me? How could I explain if he had?

"Looks like you were cleaning out the drawers," Mike said from the doorway.

Good. He wasn't questioning me. I rolled my bell bottoms and tee shirt into a ball for the laundry hamper. It was better to forget the girl I used to be. In the cold light of day, the seeds only reminded me of who I wasn't.

"I… was trying on clothes from my college days, you know, to inspire me to diet," I stammered.

"Was that on Oprah or did the old girls whip out childhood photos at dinner?" Mike asked.

"Nope. No childhood photos. For a moment, I missed the care-free days of tee shirts and jeans. The moment's over," I said, then picked up my purse and left.

7: Considerable Reality

I was glad to finish my last errand before the midday New York mugginess turned the air to soup. After three go-arounds, I spotted a parking space on a street lined with massive sycamores. By mid-August, their broken bark littered the sidewalks, a foreshadowing of fall. September, with its hideous anniversary, was fast approaching.

Silvery wind chimes announced my arrival. The herb shop, scarcely larger than my sons' bedroom, was lined with antiquated cabinetry and Lucite shelves. A red lacquer chair, its tall backrest sweeping out like a pagoda rooftop, fit neatly under a corner glass-and-brass desk. Framed hand-written signs covered a freestanding panel. I had seen those circles and lines before on the herbalist's business card. An ancient wooden cabinet standing stoically near the counter had gold brush-stroked Chinese characters on its chiseled drawers. Whether placed according to the principles of feng shui or Korean-American marketing, the furnishings looked like remnants from an Oriental rummage sale.

Herbalist Kim stood behind a dusty counter, his oily white hair threaded over his bald spot. He wore a silky black and maroon track suit that matched a tennis racket cover on the shelf behind him. I put the bag of packets on the counter in front of his skeletal hands. Instead of a greeting, he tipped his chin down in my direction. Maybe this was hello in herbal-eze.

"A friend bought these packets of sleep medication for me and I'm wondering if they could have drug interactions with prescriptions," I said. "Like, if a person suffered from arrhythmia and migraines, or needed anxiety medications." He stared past me. Had I interrupted his prayer time? Maybe he's blind. No, he's purposely ignoring me. Well, lucky you, Mr. Kim. I'm a baby boomer, the last generation to be taught good manners so I'll try again.

"Good morning, Mr. Kim," I began politely. "What an interesting shop. I'm hoping you can help me."

"Good morning. Nice today, *ueng*?"

I assumed ueng translated to *right*?

"Which-ee beta blocker do you take for your arrhythmia?" he asked while making notations on his iPad. His long yellowed finger nails were filed to points. "Buytl-buytl is your migraine medication? How many days a week do you take it? Xanax, you take that too, *ueng*?"

How did he know my medications?

"Mr. Kim, I was only going to ask if occasionally, when I can't fall asleep, I may take a packet." Why did I say that? I should have just told him to take them back.

"Did you ask your physicians if occasionally, when you suffer pain and anxiety, you can take their pills?" he cackled another question.

I was taken aback by his smarminess. I didn't need a skinny version of Kim Jong Il grilling me. "Mr. Kim, I'd like to return them. I'm disturbed by…"

"What concerned you?" he interrupted.

Concern didn't begin to describe the heartache of not finding Luke or the unfathomable lightness that followed. "Many things," my voice thinned to a whisper.

"Things you saw, Missus?"

"What I saw? Oh, so that's the side effect, right. *Ueng*. Because for a minute I thought I really was…I mean the dream was very real," I was embarrassed by my childlike reply.

"All dreams are real, Missus."

"Mrs. Pleasance. I'm Alice Pleasance," I introduced myself.

30

"Missus Alice, why do you think dreams are pretend?"

Was he toying with me? "Mr. Kim, I live in the real world. When morning comes, my considerable reality is just as I left it."

"*Ah, ueng, ueng,* nightmares don't necessarily end with daybreak. Do you live in a bad dream, Missus Alice?" he asked.

"My son, Luke was a police officer." It was not my habit to share my son's murder with strangers yet here I was confiding to an ancient tennis player in an herb shop that looked like the set from a Charlie Chan movie. "He was killed on 9/11."

My pulse quickened. A hot flash gave away my aching heart.

Mr. Kim handed me two sheets of brown paper toweling to blot my forehead.

"Missus Alice, as were my ancestors, I am a *sana mudang*- a male shaman. Whether you choose to continue this herbal treatment or not, I will remain a *mudang*. But tell me, after the nightmare, wasn't what followed calming? Were you not rested this morning?" his tone had softened.

How could he know? Rushing to Luke's last night forced me to relive those horrific hours when we still hoped he had survived yet the second dream had re-energized me. It was as though I entered a healing space.

He put his iPad on the counter next to my package. The screen-saver was a young woman with an ornate braided hair piece sitting atop her blonde hair. There was something familiar about her. Maybe I had seen her portrait in a museum.

"Actually, Mr. Kim, except for a momentary headache, I was rested." I attempted another quick peek at the picture. The screen went black.

"And your dreams?" He folded his hands on the counter. His stained talons clicked when they touched.

"I don't usually sleep very well. I can't remember the last time I had dreams. But, after I took the seeds, the things I saw and the things I felt....they were so real. I've stored them like actual memories," I confided.

"*Ah, geu re.* That is good. Some customers only see the mundane," he said. "They don't appreciate their heart's secret space."

My heart's secret space? It was a perfect description of last night's second dream. Maybe it wouldn't hurt to use the seeds every now and then, a couple of nights a week at the most. Sleeping pills were probably more dangerous than teeny organic seeds.

"Missus Alice," the *mudang* tapped his pinkie nail on the counter. "Is there something more you want to tell me?"

Was there? Refilling my heart sounded so much better than tossing and turning all night. I would keep the seeds. I snatched my package off the counter. "The sky was red."

Chapter

8: My Little Life

I called Laura from my car. She had recently taken a part-time office job not far from the herbalist's shop. It didn't bring in much money but it kept her busy. I knew she missed her step-daughter, even if she wouldn't talk about it.

"Are you at work?" I hoped she'd have time for lunch. "We can meet at my house for a bite." It was a perfect excuse to learn what she knew about Mr. Kim. Laura was a bargain-hunting authority. She must have wangled a free sample to try before she bought those seeds. What had she seen?

"No, I was off today," she said. "Let's meet at the Omega Diner. There was an estate sale in Great Neck. I stopped at your house, but Mike told me you were out. Wait until you see the fabulous things I picked up for you. You won't believe I only spent ten dollars."

I didn't share Laura's passion for cheap deals. For me, local estate sales were simply pastimes for those of us too poor to play golf but too snobby to go bowling. Besides, my forays into other lives were bittersweet. Ghosts in those age-beaten homes reminded me that eventually a young picker would look through the wake of my little life and offer ten dollars for things I once treasured.

무궁화

Laura's white summer shift complimented her olive skin. Had she lost weight? I sucked in my belly while we hugged hello. Why was she dressed up?

Our waitress placed two Lipton teabags on a saucer next to Laura's spoon. "Finally, you're getting it right," she announced loud enough to be heard by our server and the couple in the next booth. "You serve unlimited coffee refills for the price of one, why not unlimited tea?"

I thought she had a valid point but being rude to the person who could spit in our food behind the swinging doors was never a good idea. I was extra polite when I ordered the chicken noodle soup.

"Alice, look at this hobnail creamer," Laura's eyes twinkled as she unwrapped her prize, "Two dollars and not one chip." She reached deeper into her shopping bag. "But, tada! This Derby Dan cookie jar was the find of the day. I got the seller down to eight dollars for you."

Its jaunty black lid and silly bug eyes made me smile. Laura was a super picker.

"This is adorable." I handed her a ten. "And I can always use a spare creamer."

"But you told me you needed a hobnail creamer," Laura said in that I'm-right-you're-wrong tone of hers.

"Actually, I was looking for the ice cream spoon holder," I said as I placed my napkin on my lap. "I have the creamer. Luke got it for me the year I started collecting milk glass. He asked you what I wanted for Christmas. Remember?"

She squirted hand cleanser into her palm and massaged it in, then applied more and rubbed harder. Like most of my friends, Laura was uncomfortable when I talked about Luke, but why did she go all Lady Macbeth on me just for mentioning him? Our waitress brought my soup and Laura's tuna salad on rye.

Laura removed the tomato slices from her sandwich, took two huge bites then made a face. "No taste at all," she reached for the salt and knocked over the pepper shaker. Her strabismus was definitely getting worse with age. As usual, she sprinkled a few grains over her shoulder. I righted the shaker for her. "I bet the seeds helped you sleep last night," she said as she plowed through her lunch.

"Did you ever try them?" I tried to sound nonchalant.

"I don't have problems sleeping, but I tried them for you. Put me right to sleep," she isolated an onion bit in the salad and spit it into her napkin. "They're really healthy, a hundred percent all natural."

"Horse manure is all natural too, but we don't eat it," I said then wished I hadn't. When our kids were small, she covered for me in our car pool whenever I had doctor appointments with Will. Even Mike seemed to like her and he barely tolerated my other friends. Not to mention, she had just found that cookie jar for me. I let her go on about upcoming sales till we finished lunch.

"Did you have weird dreams the night you took them?" I asked. "Did you sleep walk?"

Laura lifted her tea bag from her cup and began twirling the string around the spoon. "Well, I didn't know how to tell you… but I dreamt about Luke. He was showing me his new house. He seemed happy."

Why did Laura have to say Luke was in her dream? I knew she was fond of Luke. When he was a cub scout, she'd call him her little soldier. But Luke was my son. Shouldn't I have found him in my dream? I put my napkin beside my bowl and looked for the waitress. None of this made sense. My pile of clothes in the boys' room was real. Mike saw it too. Had Laura really seen Luke?

My eyes welled-up. She put her hand over mine and we remained attached in silence. What Laura and I had witnessed were only dreams. No Korean hocus-pocus could bring Luke home.

"You OK?" She squeezed my hand before letting go.

"I'll be fine."

"I've got to make a quick stop at the restroom." Laura placed nine dollars and thirty one cents on the table. "This is for my share." She buried the extra tea bag into her purse before flagging our waitress.

Alone with my thoughts, I became aware of the temperature dropping. Had the diner suddenly gotten colder or was I coming down with something? I rubbed my arms for warmth.

"Will that be all?" Our waitress drew a smiley face next to the total. "You got chills? Means somebody just walked over your grave, hon." She tore the bill from her pad and handed it to me. "You should spit three times for protection."

I grew up in the assurance that God would bring me safely to his kingdom. Why would I need protection? I asked myself, but I already knew the answer. It took weeks before they could identify Luke's remains. Searching in vain for him again terrified me. I put my palm over my mouth. Ptui, ptui, ptui.

Chapter

9: Into the Woods

Mike was in our bed for the second night in a row. Had the air conditioner in the den broken down again? I hid a seed packet and a kid-sized juice box in my night stand drawer, lay down on top of the covers and peeked at him every five minutes till he fell asleep. *Finally!* I downed the seeds with an orange-pineapple chaser.

In an hour I awoke as young Alice. Mike's metered breaths convinced me it was safe to head down two flights of stairs to the laundry room. Even fresh from the dryer, my bell bottoms and tee shirt looked their age. Eventually, I'd have to get new clothes.

Dressed and daubed with a little lip gloss, I raced up to the kitchen and out the door.

The fog whipped through the trees dampening everything in its path. I held the car door handle. Where was I headed? Luke wasn't in Bayside. It would be fruitless to walk through his neighborhood again. There was certainly no unfinished business at the Blue Moon or with John. No need to go there.

As they did the night before, my car's headlights brightened the swarming droplets. Purple, puce, lavender, each one orbited on its own yet mingled together within the brume, reminding me of a place I could go with the flow and yet be on my own—Manhattan.

Even in another world, I wasn't daring enough to drive into the city so I headed north to the Long Island Railroad. A Wakie-the-

Rooster sign looked down over Little Neck Parkway. As I passed the Expressway service road, another giant sign lit up. A bear cub with nightcap and blanket put his finger to his pursed lips: "Winkie says: Shhh! Nassau County Line— Exits 33–39 are in Second Watch."

Why are those signs everywhere?

At the railway station parking lot, a recorded message played through hidden speakers reminding commuters that after midnight, west and eastbound trains would stop at zones in First Watch only. This was getting weird. What if my day-world money couldn't get me a ticket? I fed a twenty into the vending machine and tapped "round trip" on the keyboard. My ticket and three singles dropped into the bin. A few minutes later, I was on the 12:33 to Penn Station.

A young woman in a silk skirt that only just covered her bottom got on in Bayside and sat across from me. Five of her fingernails were painted white, five were black. She began texting.

Will my new phone work here? I certainly couldn't call home and wake up Mike. I tried my twenty-four hour pharmacy number. A message told me my call had failed. I tried the local supermarket, "Your call has failed." What was I doing wrong? The woman with the zebra fingernails thumped her cell phone several times on her knee.

"Dang! Can I borrow yours? I'm supposed to meet up with friends," she said.

I handed her my phone.

If she gets through, will I? And what do I say if someone answers? Hello. I'm somewhere in a time warp or alternate universe. Can you hear me now?

While she tapped the buttons, I took in her face. She was younger than my sons, maybe twenty-something with an attractive round face and Asian brown eyes. Had I dreamed up a Korean because of *Mudang* Kim?

"Hey, Samantha, didn't you get my text?" she shouted over the din of the train. "I'll pick you up at Three—Second Watch, tomorrow."

38

My phone worked, but I had no one in my dream world to call.

"Are you getting out at Penn?" she asked as she returned my cell.

I nodded.

"Want to share a cab? Uptown or down?"

I only had forty dollars and no idea if Visa cards were really accepted everywhere, but I answered, yes. "Sure, we can share a ride."

"Awesome, but like…where are you headed?" she raised her perfectly feathered eyebrows.

Should I try Luke's precinct? He wouldn't be there at this time of night. He avoided the city when he wasn't on duty. Besides, what if I found him here? I'd only have to leave him when I woke up. Wouldn't I?

"I'm not sure," I answered. "I guess I just wanted to get out of the house."

"I'm going to a party uptown if you want to come. I'm Chrissy Chen." She whipped out a business card from a red silk pouch and handed it to me. We shook hands limply, girl-style.

"I'm Alice Seaton." I gave my birth name.

"I work for my Mom." Chrissy explained as if I had asked. "She owns Pandam, Chinatown's number one export business. She's the CEO. I'm just hired help."

"You're Chinese?"

"I'm *American*. My parents were born here," she pointed out.

"I'm sorry. I didn't mean anything. I thought you might be Korean. It's just that I met someone the other day. He used a Korean word. Anyway, I wanted to know what it meant," I rushed to explain.

"Korean? I'm Wakie-Mad crazy for Korean food. I eat in K-town like once a month. But for Wakie-sake, stay away from Korean guys. Their mothers raise them like they're princes in their own TV dramas. One of my girlfriends dated this K-boy once. His mother said her breasts were too small! Seriously?

Everyone knows Chinese girls have bigger boobs than Korean girls," Chrissy pointed to her breasts for emphasis.

What was I supposed to say to that? I didn't need to comment. She spent the next ten minutes enumerating the perils of working with family.

"Thanks for letting me unload. You're a good listener. So what was the Korean word?" she asked.

I wondered if her conversations with strangers were always all over the place. "*Mudang*. I was told it means shaman but it probably just means herbalist," I said.

"Never heard it. Or didn't listen. I know how to say fuck you— *shee bah lah*. No, maybe that's scumbag. I'm going uptown to the AAWIB gala at Fendi. The champ's free if you want to come too," she said.

I bet champs meant champagne. Maybe I was getting the hang of being young again. "Sure." I was off to a gala without an invitation, wearing the same outfit I'd worn the night before. Why not?

We were welcomed by a line of tuxedoed males who were remarkably dashing and most definitely gay. The Fendi charity event for the Asian-American Women in Business was sumptuous—snow-white sweaters trimmed in rabbit alongside plush coats with silver beading in between skeins of chinchilla. How will I ever shop in Queens again?

"Alice, let me have your cell." Chrissy held my phone, tapping the keyboard with her thumbs. Her dexterity was fascinating. Her cell rang.

"Now we're hooked," she said. "In case we want to network." She spotted a friend on the other side of the store and excused herself with a promise to be right back.

I was ensconced in racks of buttery fall fashion wools when Chrissy returned with a flute of champagne for me. "Hey, there's a better party at MOCA, Alice. Want to come?"

It was tempting, but still, "I can't tonight." I apologized.

"That's OK. Next week there's an event at Red Egg. We can meet up at the LIRR and head in together." Her friends waved for us to follow. "I'll text you," she called back as she joined them.

A rack of cream colored angora cardigans caught my eye. I fingered through the sleeves, luxuriating in their downy nap till a salesman peered over his rhinestone reading glasses and rushed over. His professionally tightened cheeks would have made Laura jealous. "*Pippi*, what are you dressed in? You look like the love child of Daisy Mae and Timothy Leary." He pulled out a dove grey micro-mini skirt. "Try this on to show off those great long legs."

"Thanks." I flashed a smile. The last time I had the face and figure to look great in anything, the style was ankle length peasant skirts and cheap beads. Who knew that at 62 I'd get to show off my legs?

The Fendi's tag was marked $1250. For a skirt? Even if I looked like a super model in it, it was $1,200 over my budget.

"Thanks, but not tonight," I said and put my empty glass on a display case. "Is there a place nearby where I can get a quiet drink?"

"Exit, make a right, three doors down, called Vintage, straight and upscale, you could do worse," he put his finger to his lips.

I probably had.

10: The Great Pretender

As soon as I walked in, I knew what the salesman meant by upscale. With its polished oak bar and classic rock music, Vintage did not cater to the Levis and t-shirt crowd, but rather, as my mother would say, "These people are the smart set."

Young men in European suits clutched blackberries like they were extensions of their Rolex-wrapped wrists. Those who weren't talking on their phones were texting.

The women were indistinguishable from one another, all of them dressed Manhattan-style—black boy-cut pants and matching blazers. They tossed their designer bags onto the bar like knapsacks. I clutched my jumble-sale satchel to my chest. Assuming that the drinks were probably as pricey as the clothes in Fendi's, I'd splurge on one glass of wine, enjoy the music, and then leg it back to Penn Station.

I took the first available bar stool and hummed along to Carol King and Gloria Gaynor. How long had it been since I slow-danced in a man's arms?

A new set began. It was the Platters and I couldn't help lip-syncing, "In a world of my own."

The barstool next to mine changed owners. My new neighbor looked like John Travolta in *Saturday Night Fever* and smelled like peaches. His silk shirt, opened at the collar, revealed a fringe of chest hair and a weighty gold cross. He made a purposeful hand gesture to show off a large solitaire on his pinky, ordered two Fuzzy Navels and pushed one in my direction. The scent of peaches grew stronger. I faced the man who just bought my drink. There were two patrons who didn't fit in with the Vintage crowd; me, in my resurrected cotton and denim and him.

"Thank you." I raised my glass.

"I'm Michelangelo Medici. What's your name?"

"I'm Elizabeth… the Second," I shot back.

"Smart girl. Names aren't important. Last night I was Pietro Gigante. You collect old records?" He didn't give me time to answer. "I watched you mouthing to *The Great Pretender*. Most people here never heard of the Platters or even Freddie Mercury. But you knew all the lyrics."

"Are you a vinyl collector?" I asked although he didn't look like the nerdy album collectors Laura and I met at estate sales.

"I don't collect records. I'm into bigger things," he jammed a ten into the tip glass.

I stifled a yawn. Bigger things? Names are not important? I'm starting to think he's "The Great Pretender." Even in my dreams, single bars were still the same—over-priced drinks and under-developed men.

He took out his wallet and flipped to a photo. "I collect cars."

The picture showed him behind the wheel of a '69 GTO convertible. Next to him was a golden-haired mixed breed. He couldn't be all bad. He had a dog.

I told him about our old setter-mix, Ginger. He talked about his first dog, Rex. We toasted, "To mutts and animal shelters!" Then had two more rounds.

"I have my Aston-Martin around the corner," he offered.

I caught his drift but leaving wasn't a bad idea. I didn't have enough money to linger by myself. Sure, he was a total stranger who wouldn't tell me his name, but I couldn't assume he was homicidal. Besides, I had to walk over twenty blocks back to Penn Station.

무궁화

The Great Pretender led me inside a tiered parking lot that stretched to the end of the street. I looked up at two massive rows of elevator skeletons. Each one held a parked car. A chain link gate fortified with barbwire coils served as a warning to all would-be car thieves. It also cautioned me. Why did I leave the bar with a man I had only talked with for a few hours?

"Thanks for walking me outside, but I'm going to pass on the ride," I gently delivered my change of heart.

"Don't worry. You're safe. It's my parking lot in both worlds. I bought this and another one up in the Bronx in the seventies. When I started traveling twenty years ago, I bought them here too," he said.

"Maybe those Fuzzy Navels soaked my brain but did you say *the seventies?*" He certainly had my attention now.

"I did. I bought the lots over thirty years ago and like I said, I bought them again. A good investment is a good investment," he used his pointer finger like a teacher.

A car alarm howled from its far off steel cage then, just as suddenly, went silent. The place was creepy, but I was riveted by his declaration. "You're saying you bought this lot thirty years ago?" I asked again.

"Why? Do I look too young for that? How old do I look to you?" he jutted his chin.

Other than his outfit, he looked the same age as the other young men in Vintage. His face was getting increasingly closer to mine. I took in his full dark brows and thick lips and stepped backwards. "Twenty… six?"

"Bingo! Twenty-six. That's what my *mudang* promised the seeds would do. So far, so good," he said with a grin.

Mudang? Did he mean an herbalist like Mr. Kim? I was afraid to ask.

"I know what you're thinking." He sounded so sure of himself. "It just dawned on you that this isn't a dream," he waited for my answer.

This has to be a dream, I thought, and if I have any sense at all, I will force myself to wake up. "I'll be going now," I said aloud.

"This is all real, you know," he said. "I could tell who you were as soon as you walked into Vintage. One whiff of that peach smell and I knew I'd found a fellow traveler."

"The peach fragrance at the bar?" I breathed in. The orchard smell remained fresh. "This scent is from the seeds?"

"It's cuz the seeds contain the same proteids as peaches," he said. "At least that's what I think my *mudang* said. I'm not into chemistry. The main thing is that people here can't detect it, but he promised me that I would smell it if I met another traveler. That's how I knew who you were."

"Are you saying we, you and I, actually travel to this place? And you've been doing it for twenty years?" I could hear the fear in my voice.

"Yup." He pulled out a cigarette from his pack and lit it. "Started on January 24, 1989. Do you know what tickles my balls the most?" He tilted his head back to exhale. "The women I met when I first came here, they're in their forties now, probably looking for their own fountains of youth."

That was more than I wanted to know about him, but I needed to learn more about the seeds. "So I'm twenty-six too? Why am I so young here?"

"Didn't your *mudang* explain it?" He took another drag.

Herbalist Kim hadn't explained anything to me. "Actually, my mudang wasn't very forthcoming," I said.

"*Mudangs* are like that. They're all connected by maternal blood lines. I think it makes some of them a little screwy," he exhaled a slender plume of smoke. "Anyways, we just don't come here young. We stay young as long as we don't go to sleep. A sleepover here is a ticket with no backsies. So, don't spend the night. And speaking of spending, the money here is the same as ours but don't even think about using your credit card and whatever you do, pay attention to the watch zone signs," his tone had changed.

"The ones with the cute cartoon bears and roosters?" I asked.

"Cute? Don't you know anything about this place?" He shook

his head in disbelief. "OK blue-eyes, here's a free tutorial. We can discuss how you'll show your gratitude later," he said with a smile that un-nerved me even more. "We're in an alternate universe, but that doesn't mean it's an identical twin of ours. Some things are definitely different, like that incessant red sky," he pointed his finger up to the heavens. "The economy seems to lag a few years behind ours. That's something I pay attention to, but the biggest difference I saw was after 9/11," he added.

My stomach knotted. Did I really want to hear about 9/11 from this man?

The Great Pretender flicked his cigarette onto the asphalt. "In 2002, their police commissioner created a grid that redistricted the boroughs into two watch zones. A minute after midnight until noon is First Watch. A minute after noon till midnight is Second Watch. One watch is quiet while the other one is working, eating, screwing-whatever. Then they switch. It's like the London blackouts in WWII. Zone cops patrol the Winkie zones. Regular cops patrol the Wakies," he said.

"People here are OK with that?" This certainly wasn't identical to my world.

"You'll see. Folks here are easy going. They feel it keeps them safe. I'm not about to tell them I'm safe in my world without their zones," he snickered.

"What if I leave New York?" I asked, knowing full well I wasn't even gutsy enough to drive into Manhattan.

"All of this America is zoned now. Europe and most of Asia are too. If you enter a zone when it's Winkie time, the cops will clock you, even a pretty girl like you – so don't screw up, and remember what I said about falling asleep," he took a step towards me. "I don't fall asleep here," he said. "Cuz' I don't cuddle and drop off after sex." With that, he pulled me in for a kiss.

I wriggled out of his hold. I may have looked twenty-six but sixty-two years of experience had taught me that I don't have to stay anywhere I don't want to.

11: The Year of the Ox

Indian summer was soon replaced by fall rain. I hadn't celebrated autumn in nearly a decade. It heralded my time of mourning. I had forbidden myself any reminiscences of happy Halloweens or apple picking Saturdays. The 9/11 memorial observation, like the changing seasons, had also come and gone. But that year, I declined to participate.

Oak and Elm leaves painted the sidewalks in gypsy colors till the first nippy gusts of winter blew them away. I watched snow fall softly on Christmas Eve but couldn't recall if I saw that here or there.

Since I began travelling, my seed doses were random, two, sometimes three times a week. I flourished as young Alice in the place I'd come to call Red Sky; with indoor rock climbing down on Grand Street, catching *Spiderman* at Foxwoods, and shopping everywhere. But the real me was growing weaker. My complexion had taken on a ghostly pallor. I had to drag myself out of bed most mornings to choke down my headache meds and then last week, after a night out with Chrissy in Red Sky, I couldn't get out of bed at all.

The sour taste of morning mouth woke me up.

"Dad, Mom's up," my son called out. "Mom, are you better now? You are, right?""

Wasn't it a workday? Why was Will here? "I'm a little sleepy," I answered.

"You can't be sleepy. You've been sleeping all week," he theorized, but I saw the fear in his eyes.

"Just a touch of flu. I'm on the mend, really. As soon as I wash up, I'll make breakfast," I said as perkily as I could muster.

Like most mornings that winter, I avoided the mirror while I brushed my teeth. I didn't want to be reminded of the terrible toll travelling had taken on my body. Unfortunately, when I raised my head to gargle, my reflection caught me. Dear Lord, what have the seeds done? My hair was capped with an inch of mousy grey. Even my eyebrows had whitened. No more traveling for me.

I threw on my robe and headed downstairs. "Do you guys want apple juice or orange?" Mike and Will eyed me as if I was an apparition while I served up juice and cereal.

"Mom, if you feel better…. Maybe you should get your hair fixed." Will noted shyly.

For Will to notice, I must really look like crap.

"I'm sorry I made you worry. I guess I must have seemed pretty sick," I assured him while pouring Mike's coffee.

Mike scratched at his morning stubble. "You got up to shower, eat and use the bathroom, but mostly you were the walking dead." The skin beneath his beard reddened.

"Mom isn't any kind of dead. Are you Mom?" Will's anxiety over my health was escalating.

"It's an expression. Mom's fine now. For God's sake, Alice, tell him you're fine," Mike snapped at me.

"Of course I'm fine. It'll take more than a little flu bug to hurt me."

Why was Mike so jumpy? Had he seen me leave at night? Good grief, maybe they both watched me disappear. "Will, did you stay here last night?" I treaded lightly.

"No. I came at 7:30," Will explained. "The other days I had to go to work and Monday, Ruthie and I went to the movies. Ruthie likes Brad Pitt."

This was the second time he'd mentioned Ruthie. I remembered the family. Ruthie's father was a pastor. The family moved away to serve at a permanent mission in Africa. They'd probably go back soon. Had Will understood Ruthie was just visiting New York?

"Will, why don't you bring Ruthie to lunch next week?" I casually offered after breakfast. "I'd love to see her again. It's been more than…."

"Buy corn chips, Mom. Ruthie likes corn chips with salsa," he broke in. Then with a wave, he was off.

My eyes filled. Will had a girlfriend. Growing up, Will had met his trials with a brave heart, but I never dreamed he'd find love. When Luke died, it left Will inconsolable. For a while, I thought I'd lose him too. But eventually, he rallied. Somehow, using all his strengths, he managed to move on. Why couldn't I?

무궁화

After the encounter with my son, I decided to stay home that night. I put the kettle on for a cup of decaf in the hope of getting some real sleep. The steam began to sputter; spitting scalding drops onto the stovetop in the same pattern they always made. Why should the steam or the droplets be different? We've had the same kettle on the same stove for thirty years. Things don't change unless you change them. I shut off the heat and left the kitchen with a juice box to wash down my seeds. I refused to be marooned in my bedroom all night while Mike, as usual, snored like a walrus in the den.

By First Watch—Three a.m., Chrissy and I had in-line skated for six miles on Park Drive. We handed in our skates and headed downtown to Chelsea for hot chocolate. On the way, we approached the One Three, Luke's precinct. Since coming to Red Sky, I had made several pilgrimages to likely places to find information about my son. There was no listing of Luke Pleasance at the police academy in Gramercy Park and nothing at the Municipal Archives on Chambers Street, but as I neared the precinct that was identical to Luke's last safe haven on earth, I knew my search was not over.

We were just a few feet away from its steel doors. Had a Red Sky Luke put on his uniform and joked with his fellow officers here on that September morning? Had he, unlike my Luke, survived? I turned my head to avoid the World Trade Center List of the Fallen next to the doorway. Of all the places I had gone to find Luke, this was the one I couldn't bring myself to enter. Until now.

"Chrissy, mind if we stop a minute?" I linked my arm through hers. I was so grateful we had met. She was my Red Sky guide and safety net. With Chrissy by my side, I felt strong enough to put the final stroke on my search for Luke. "I want to look for someone at this precinct." I told her.

She eyed two officers who were coming off Watch. "Sure. Actually, I once knew a really cute guy here," she said and elbowed my side.

Once inside, I braced myself to approach the desk. "Excuse me."

A fresh-faced black sergeant looked up from his work.

"I'm looking for an officer attached to this precinct. Sergeant Luke Pleasance?" I held my breath. *Tell me you know him. Please, please, please say he's here.*

"Never heard of him. But you can call me Luke any time you want," he flirted.

"I'll call you Luke," Chrissy piped up behind me.

"You?" He smiled broadly. "You'll probably break my heart."

My heart was breaking too.

We crossed the street to flag down a cab. Chrissy tallied the complications of dating cops while stomping her boots on the sidewalk to keep warm. I let her go on and on, nodding at appropriate times, but my thoughts were elsewhere. I had to accept that nowhere on any earth would I find my son.

A yellow taxi pulled up. "Thank God," Chrissy said as she opened the door.

"Yes," I agreed. It was time to release Luke to his rightful place in heaven.

무궁화

The next morning, I awakened before the alarm, leaped out of bed and called my hair salon. Calm and rested, I gossiped with my stylist and treated myself to a French manicure. I felt like a new woman as I made my way to the herb shop. *Get ready, Mudang Kim. I have lots of questions.*

The herbalist stood behind his counter drinking tea from a small metal cup. While his parchment skin and greased hair hadn't changed during my absence, his maroon track suit had been replaced with a green one. Snow skis leaned on the same counter that held a tennis racket the last time I visited.

"Missus Alice, *uh soh oh se yo*. Welcome," he called to me.

"*Mudang* Kim, nice to see you again."

"Did you come for refills?" he wiped his mouth with the back of his hand.

Refills? Ah, the moment of truth. "Yes," I said.

The *mudang* led me to the ornate cabinet at the end of the counter. The afternoon sunlight buffed the brass draw pulls till they shined. I put on my readers for a better look. The pulls were intricately carved gold fish with delicate scales and sorrowful eyes. He grabbed one of the fish by its belly and pulled the drawer open.

"Mr. Kim, is it possible I need a smaller dosage?" I asked, presuming there was probably no cure for magic seed addiction.

"Are you not enjoying your nights?" he answered with a question.

"My nights aren't the problem, but up until recently your seeds made me sick during the day," I said. "They aren't dangerous are they?"

He took a handful of packets from the drawer and tossed them into the center of a silk scarf. Like dust in an attic, their musk hung in the air tickling my nose till I sneezed.

"Missus Alice, everything we feel can be dangerous. Everything we know can be dangerous," he said. "We know how to eat, yet some of us eat ourselves to an early grave, *guh rhu chee?*"

Was he purposely talking in riddles? "Yes. *Groo-chee*," I parroted back. "Still, in the beginning…they left me exhausted."

"I will tell you this, Missus Alice. Over the years I have seen many seed eaters. Most arrive with years of heavy burdens, expecting me to lighten their loads in a night. Some look for things they know can't be found. But only a very few learn that what cannot be regained is still available in the heart." He smoothed the corners of the scarf with his palms. "Acceptance is most restorative."

Mudang Kim had just described me. I guess I always knew Luke wasn't in Red Sky. It was time to stop searching.

"By now, your side effects have stopped, haven't they?" he asked.

How does he know everything? "You're right," I said. "They have."

He stacked the packets into two even columns. "Perhaps your unpleasant symptoms won't return."

I had more questions. "*Mudang* Kim, is it possible for someone from this world to see me change?"

"Anything is possible." He lifted two of the scarf's silk corners and knotted them tightly at the top of the packets.

Very enlightening. Why was I trying to get straight answers from a man who sells dreams for a living? I took one last stab at it. "Please, *Mudang* Kim, I'd like to know if my husband wakes up, will he see a young me?"

He took his time tying a second knot before handing me the silk tote. "Your husband will see what he wants to see."

What's that supposed to mean?

The *mudang* reached down below the counter and lifted a large packing box without even a groan. I wondered what seeds he chomped on to make him so strong.

He taped the box shut and lifted it high above his head to top off a pillar of other boxes. "Missus Alice, I am leaving for Korea. I won't return till long after *Seollal*, the New Year."

"How long will you be gone?"

He closed his eyes and spoke as if beginning an incantation. "The Year of the Earth Ox begins next month. In my home town, the women will scrub their kitchens, cook up steaming pots of *man doo guk*, and leave the lights burning in all the rooms. No one will sleep that first night. To sleep will mean waking up with snow-white eyebrows in the morning."

How could he know about my eyebrows? Unless, all seed takers eventually wake up that way. Why can't he just say what he means?

His eyes opened wide. "This shop will be closed till summer."

"Closed? Are there other places that sell the seeds? Should I take a case home?" I asked, trying not to give away my panic.

"If you're concerned, I will give you six months' worth today," he said as he lifted the top off a wooden crate.

Inside were small white linen pillows each holding twelve packets. Every pillow was tied with twine that wrapped around the neighboring pillow as well. There seemed no end to his supply. He picked out a twine loop and raised it from the carton. His sharpened fingernail cut a crescent into one of the pillows, puncturing a packet. Several tiny seeds fell into the underside of his nail.

Six months' worth would be more than enough, I thought. I go to Red Sky only two times a week. OK, maybe three. But I could pace myself. Anyway, I have to go tonight. Chrissy and I are meeting at a new place in Midtown. "How much do I owe you for the refills?" I opened my wallet.

He flicked the seeds into his cup and slurped down the rest of his tea. "Refills are free with the first purchase," he chortled like a cartoon ogre.

I was stunned by his answer. Even though I accepted visiting a world where I was forty years younger, getting something free in New York City was preposterous.

Chapter

12: Borrowed Light

That night, another downy blue-red mist greeted me as I opened my kitchen door. Then, as it had all my nights of travel, floated eastward down my street until it disappeared. Alone with happy thoughts, I walked to the Union Turnpike bus stop.

I had grown accustomed to Red Sky's Watch Zones. At the corner, Wakie, the crowing rooster morphed into Winkie the Bear in his night cap. Hurry home! Second Watch ends in 30 Minutes. Time now: 11:30PM. Have a great Watch.

Grumbling thunder told me rain was on the way. I should have worn a slicker but I couldn't wait to wear the pea coat Chrissy picked out for me last week. She found it when we went to Bloomingdales on Lexington Avenue to scavenge through the dregs of the post-Christmas sales. While pawing through the holiday jewelry, Chrissy attached two sequined ornaments to her earrings and asked: "What do you think, Alice? Something a little blingier?" I snapped her photo on my phone knowing I could only view it in Red Sky. Each night was more delightful than the one before because of her friendship. She was fun to be with; eager to share her heart, yet never prying, even when I paid for things with hands full of cash.

Besides, if I hadn't met her on the train last summer, I might never had learned that my phone worked in Red Sky-even if the only person I contacted there was my one friend; Chrissy.

I listened to my voice mail to recheck her instructions.

"Alice, remember what I told you. Don't take the train. The Rapid Eastern Metro bus starts in Floral Park and ends on Third and Fifty-Seventh. That's right in front of our meeting place. You'll see a giant silver 950 on the building. Later, bestie."

I dashed across the street to catch my bus.

무궁화

Just as the bus approached 950 Third Avenue, my cell rang. "Alice, don't kill me," Chrissy began her apology, "one of our wholesalers ditched on us and my mom's having a fit. I have to work late. Are you OK to go solo tonight?"

The last time I partied alone, I ended up in a parking lot with the horny Great Pretender.

"Sure," I said. But I wanted to Red Sky people-watch and girl-talk all night. "No biggie."

"Let me make some calls. I'll round up a few friends to go with you," Chrissy tried to make things right.

"I'm fine. And I'm not a baby. We'll catch up in a few Watches."

"That's a problem because I have to go to Hong Kong next Watch. I don't know for how long," Chrissy purred. "I'll pick up a knock-off Chanel for you while I'm there. OK? Are we still friends?"

"Yes."

The sidewalk teemed with people. A Greek restaurant opened its doors for First Watch. The mingling aromas of expensive perfume and sautéed spices made an exotic cocktail.

I was on my own in Manhattan. The possibilities were endless.

Just a few feet away a young, dark-haired man stood in an opened black Chesterfield. It seemed like he was trying to coax his friend up from his seat on the curb. Even though they spoke in another language, two beer bottles on the ground announced their previous activity. Red Sky, it seemed, had no prohibitions on public drinking, even after New Year's. Apparently, I was the only one interested in the pair.

"*Hyung*, get up, you Winkie-ass jerk-off! *Aish*, every year, two beers and you act like this!" the standing man complained. He shoved his friend's head with the back of his hand. The tone reminded me of the obnoxious teasing that Will endured in middle school. I looked at the man seated on the curb as he brushed his silken hair back with his fingers. It was the handsomest face I'd ever seen. Was he famous? He could have passed for a Samurai movie actor. Definitely not the kind of man who was bullied.

"*Hyung*, get up, or I'm leaving!" his friend threatened.

Trucks roared past us in both directions. A turbaned cab driver leaned on his horn. The street noise almost drowned out their voices. Would he really leave his friend on the sidewalk? I headed in their direction.

"You're not going to leave him there, are you?" I asked.

The standing man flashed a smile before answering. "He'll be fine. He just had a couple of drinks to toast his mother's birthday."

"Why doesn't he just visit her?"

"He can't. She was killed on 9/11."

I gulped in a shard of chilled air.

"*Hyung*, get yourself together!" He nudged his friend with his knee, and turned to me. "Look, I'm wicked late." He stepped off the curb and signaled for a taxi. "Do you think you can talk him into getting up?"

I looked down at the man on the curb. "Excuse me. We need to get you out of here, Young. Is that your name? Young?" I asked.

"His name is Baek Hoon. Tell him to meet me at Pho 34 in Koreatown," the friend said.

"But I heard you call him Young. Don't jerk me around," I demanded.

"*Aee-shi*, I call him *hyung* because he's older. It's how Korean men show respect," the man explained. "But his name is Hoon. In English, his last name is Park…never mind. Just tell Hoon to call Spencer."

"You're leaving him? But it's going to rain any minute," I pointed to the swollen clouds overhead.

"He'll be all right. Mostly he wants to be alone. Believe me. I've seen him after a six pack. This is nothing." He got into his cab.

"Will you stay?" Hoon looked up at me from his seat on the curb. "Just pretend to know me." I studied his sable eyes. If I had suspected the slightest bit of insincerity, I would have left. Instead, I saw the same profound sadness I saw in myself.

I sat down next to him.

Hoon dropped his head on my shoulder. Along with growing old, I had grown up and learned a thing or two about compassion. I wrapped my arm over his back to slowly and steadily pat his shoulder.

The rain began slowly. Pedestrian umbrellas popped up like forest mushrooms and I worried he'd catch a chill if I left him there.

"I'll stay with you, Hoon. My name is Alice. You can pretend to know me too," I said softly.

When the rain picked up, Hoon stood and held his hand out to me. "My pity-party is officially over." He took off his jacket and held it over our heads. "See that coffee shop at the corner." He pointed to a red and white striped awning. "Let's make a run for it!"

The aroma of roasted beans welcomed us as we shook off the rain. Hoon secured a small round-top table with his soaked jacket while we ordered our coffees. We returned to sit on high wooden stools facing one another.

"I apologize for my behavior. I am sincerely sorry. I'm down-on-my–knees-begging-for-forgiveness sorry." Hoon lifted the lids off our paper cups to cool them. I allowed myself a long look at him. His was a face to catalogue and memorize; something to remember before going to bed.

"Do you want to talk about your mom?" I asked.

"I still miss her," he answered before placing the sugar packs between us. "She had just started her new job at Morgan Chase in the South Tower. She'd come home late at night, but she'd cook dinner and sit with me while I ate."

It was the first time I allowed another 9/11 victim to talk about his tragedy. Up until then, I hadn't been ready to let in anyone else's loss. "I'm sure your mother fought as hard as she could not to leave you," I knew I would have for my sons.

"*Yeh*, she was an absolute tiger-mom." Hoon put a stirrer into my cup. "When I was in high school, she'd check my homework at dawn. If she saw a mistake, she'd drag me out of bed and make me do it over. I was surprised she didn't put out the Tower fires and run back home to make dinner." He took his first sip. "I don't mean to burden you. I know I'm not the only person who lost someone that day."

Could I talk about Luke? I decided not yet and re-stirred my coffee.

He set his cup on the table. "OK, now that I've broken the cardinal dating rule by talking about my mother, let me charm you with my best opening," he pretended to roll up his sleeves for a hard job. "So, do you come here often?" I liked that he shut down our talk about his mom with humor.

His shirt cuff rode up his wrist to reveal a plastic NY Mets watch. Why would such a well-dressed man wear something like that? Then I remembered I bought two of those for my boys when they were twelve. I bet his mom bought that watch for him too. How young was he? Old enough to remember the '86 World Series, I hoped.

I pointed to Hoon's watch. "I'm a Mets fan, too."

His smile lit up his face. "Only eleven weeks till Opening Watch at the new Citifield. This'll be our year. Ya gotta believe."

A teenager in lime green glasses and matching ear-buds squeezed past us. Her latte dripped onto our table. Hoon and I wiped the spots with our napkins. It was so much nicer to clean up with a man than after him.

"Spencer and I have been Mets fans since we ditched school to see Pedro Martinez at Shea," Hoon said. "So, even though he left me on that nasty curb in the rain, I have to forgive him."

"Oh, I almost forgot. I jumped in, "You're supposed to meet up with Spencer in Koreatown."

"I'm in much better company now. Should we have dinner?"

Dinner? Like out on a date? "I really can't." I stood to go.

Hoon helped me on with my new coat. A bare hint of his cologne awakened feelings I thought were long dead.

"Are you sure you have to go?" he asked as he threw away our cups.

I wasn't sure of anything.

Third Avenue was enjoying a temporary lull between the start of First Watch and the 4 a.m. lunchtime. The sky had deepened to what John, the sailor I met last summer, called night-red. In its center, the full moon made a silver circle above the skyscrapers like a punch hole on a paper valentine. Below, discarded fast food wrappers floated peacefully on the curbside puddles, reminders that a storm had just swept through.

"Let me pay your cab fare home," Hoon said as he scanned Fifty Seventh Street for a taxi.

"But, I live in Queens," I protested.

"No problem. We can walk to my garage. I'll drive you back," he said.

His offer touched my heart. I brushed a swath of hair from his forehead. Hoon's eyes explored my face slowly as if we weren't parting. "*Yeh pooh dah*. You're very pretty," he said softly.

Of all the compliments I had lived long enough to hear, that one trumped them all. "I should get home," I said.

"When will I see you again?"

"I don't know. I'm not in Midtown very often," I told him. But I surely would be if I knew he was waiting.

"Alice, are you dumping me?" he asked. It was meant to be a joke but we both knew it wasn't.

"I live very far away. I'm practically from…the moon," I fell silent.

He tilted my chin towards the sky. "Standing here in the moonlight, I almost believe you."

"I once read the moon produces no light. It borrows it from the sun." My voice cracked as I spoke. *Had that sounded corny? He's so cool and I'm so not.*

"Well, whether you borrowed it or own it, moonlight suits you, Alice."

I lowered my head in embarrassment. When was the last time I was the center of attention? Was I ever?

Hoon folded his tall body till he could look up at my face. "You see, Alice-in-moonlight, you're not so far away."

13: Red Sky in Morning, Sailor's Warning

A surprise snowstorm curled up the coast from Virginia to Maine, leaving ten inches of new powder in its wake. Outside, the morning sun bounced off the snow drifts along my street like shattering glass. I squinted back at the light and remembered my night. Hoon's cologne mixed with his pheromones making him the most desirable man on earth.

I couldn't remember his last name even though his friend had said it two times. Then my morning coffee jogged my memory. *Park. Hoon Park.*

I took my laptop from the kitchen cabinet. Since it was rarely used, we shelved it next to the cookbooks. I found a site that listed the World Trade Center victims alphabetically, and scrolled down to see Luke's name.

Good morning my angel.

I rubbed the letters like I had brushed his hair from his eyes after a hard day at play. It was the way I brushed Hoon's hair last night.

I scrolled up. *Gye Hyong Park—age 28—worked for Metropolitan Life—killed in the North Tower.* She was much too young to have been Hoon's mother but there were no other Parks on the list.

Oh what a dope I was. That young man was another Great Pretender. Figuring out how to rest his head near my cleavage just made him cleverer.

Still, I couldn't believe that Hoon was a fraud. I remembered his warm hand on my chin. I must have misheard his friend.

Mike, in his underwear and groggy from sleep, walked past my chair without a nod or greeting. He stretched till his curly chest hairs lifted and drooped. I turned back to the screen. When had we stopped saying, good morning? After a substantial yawn, he leaned over my shoulder to snoop. "Looking up something?"

"Nothing really." I snapped the top down and returned the computer to its cabinet.

"Since you're up, mind getting me a coffee?" he asked.

He had just walked past the coffee pot but he couldn't pour himself a cup? Why was I getting angry at Mike? Wasn't I always the coffee bearer? In truth, my irritation had nothing to do with Mike. I felt guilty thinking about the young man in Red Sky.

"Mike, why don't we walk down to Ridders Pond," I emptied the pot and then adjusted the kitchen blinds to admire the frosted drifts outside. A blast of fresh air would put me right. "Remember how we'd pack the boys and Ginger into the car to watch the snow geese on the ice?" I brought his coffee to the table. "Luke and Will loved chasing Ginger in the snow."

"I didn't love finding frozen dog poop in the yard," Mike grumbled as he headed for the front door to retrieve the Daily News off the top step. "At least the paper boy made it through. Must be a foot out there. Sky's nice though, really dark pink."

"What would you say if I told you I dreamt the sky was red?" I asked.

"Let me think. Was it a morning red like the one we have now?"

"No It was late at night," I remembered it well.

"Then that's OK. Remember, red sky at night, sailors' delight." Mike tucked the newspaper under his arm and left for the bathroom.

I put up a fresh pot and watched the neighborhood from my window. Across the street, the Novak kids were already building their front lawn snowman. Their Mom dashed out in snow boots and a ski parka over her nightgown to bring them a carrot nose.

I rapped on my window pane. Jeanette waved back and instructed her brood to do the same. Until I discovered Red Sky, I often envied her energy. Now I was more impressed by the way she used it. Her husband had recently been deployed to Afghanistan, and she'd taken on all his chores from mowing the lawn in summer to decking the house with Christmas lights last December. I watched as she ringed the snowman's neck with her scarf.

There's still fun in the world, I thought. Mike and I should join in.

I sat at the kitchen table till my second cup cooled. When had it snowed? There had been a stinging rain for a short while in Red Sky. That's when Hoon and I ducked in for coffee. But it wasn't cold enough to freeze.

"It's amazing how quickly the snow piled up," I called towards the bathroom door.

"Quickly?" Mike, newspaper under his arm, exited to the flourish of the flushing toilet behind him. "It's been snowing like a son of a bitch since midnight," he said.

"I don't suppose you'd like to make snow angels?" It was a backward invitation; the kind used by shy teenaged boys and long-suffering wives.

"In the yard?"

"Well, that's where the snow is. We could have a snowball fight. I'll help you build a fort," I offered.

"It's freezing outside."

"Just ten minutes."

I took in Mike's pasty complexion and graying hair. He'll turn sixty-five in May, but he looks older. That permanent five o'clock shadow doesn't help. I wonder what Hoon will look like at Mike's age. One thing's for sure, Hoon's chiseled chin didn't have enough facial hair to make a gray beard.

"Forget it, Alice, that's ten minutes on top of the hour it'll take me to snow-blow the damn driveway," he said and went upstairs to dress.

I was washing our coffee cups when he took his parka and ski hat from the front hall closet and headed outside.

As soon as the door closed, I slipped on my boots and followed his path to the garage. "Take that you varmint!" I lobbed a hard-packed sinker at his back, but missed.

"You are messing with the wrong guy," he yelled back. He cupped a handful of snow from the hedge and hit my shoulder. Game on!

We trampled the drifts scooping out fists full of crystals for weapons. Mike's snowballs hit me five times to each of my sinkers until a pillow of snow slipped from a pine branch onto my head. I shook off the freezing confetti. The fresh air had done its job. My outlook was brighter. "Let's make two angels before we go in!" I waved my arms like wings.

"Not so fast!" Mike pulled me down to the ground. "Who won the great snowball match today?" He climbed on top of me and brandished a snowball above our heads. "Who is the once and future snowball king? Wrong answer and you'll eat snow!"

We hadn't been so fun-loving in years.

Laura opened her upstairs window and leaned out. Her head and hair made a Gorgon's silhouette against the sanguine morning sky. "Well, look who feels young enough to play in the snow," she called down to us.

Her words were more condemnation than snappy greeting.

Mike dropped his snowball. He stood up without as much as a nod in Laura's direction. "Let's go inside. I'm cold," he said as he headed back into the house.

I got up off the hardened snow by myself.

Chapter

14: Love like A Fool

The bus ride into Midtown reminded me of the time my boys, then eight, were loudly counting down the seconds till our Disney World jitney arrived at the Magic Kingdom.

"Are we there yet?" they asked over and over in unison.

"Be patient," I instructed. "We'll be there in an instant."

Luke tugged on my sleeve. "But, Mom, sometimes instant gratification isn't fast enough."

I finally appreciated Luke's wisdom. I couldn't get to the place where I met Hoon fast enough. The wait had my heart pumping as though I had run all the way from Queens. As soon as the bus pulled up to its last stop, I jumped off to scan the crush of workers heading for the bus queues.

An army of commuters were climbing up from the IND subway station. I studied their faces as well. A bearded man in a black hoodie stared back. What was I thinking? This may be Red Sky but it's still Manhattan. Girls in short skirts are lunatic magnets. I scurried towards the safety of the 950 entrance.

The Change-of-Watch crowds were thinning. What made me think Hoon would return to look for me too? He probably had a girlfriend. I recalled his high cheekbones and skin the color of tupelo honey. He probably had a fan club.

The wind picked up, bringing the unmistakable January damp. My denim skirt left my legs shivering and my peep-toed heels were more fashionable than functional. I pulled up on my scarf for warmth.

"*Ja gi ya!* My Alice from the moon." Hoon was seated on the bus bench where we had said goodnight.

This was really too good to be true. The seeds must have produced episodic dreams. Why else would I meet the only man in two universes who stayed right where I left him?

He looked taller than I'd remembered and much leaner than my husband and sons. His eyelids stretched taut over his eyes; making him both alluring and impelling.

"*Bo guh ship ugh suh*. I missed you, Alice. I'm really glad you came back from the moon." His smile framed beautiful white teeth. "Let's eat. I'm starving," he invited.

I wasn't the least bit hungry but I would have eaten boiled snakes to be near him.

He suggested Nino's on 52nd. We walked five blocks along Third Avenue. By the time we reached the restaurant, Hoon had taken my hand in his.

Nino's foyer was flanked by two marble columns that rose off plush maroon carpeting. I tried not to gawk at the impeccably out-fitted wait staff or the gleaming stemware. I hadn't seen flower arrangements that grand since my cousin's wedding. The maître d' greeted Hoon warmly and led us to a corner table.

The sommelier arrived. "Did you want the 2006 Marchesi di Barola tonight, Mr. Park?"

Hoon looked to me for approval. Me? I thought wines only had three names—white, red and rosé. I nodded yes.

Our waitress described the evening's specials.

We ordered yellow beet, tomato and buffalo mozzarella in a balsamic reduction for our appetizers. I was impressed by menus that weren't covered in plastic and grateful for an English mother who taught me table manners. Did Hoon dine out every night? I can't even remember the last time Mike and I ate in a Manhattan restaurant. I should be ashamed, dining like a Roman while Mike's home alone. I'd have to make it up to him somehow.

My entree was a perfectly charred red snapper circled by fanned fingerling potatoes and baby carrot tournees the size of Christmas bulbs. Hoon insisted I taste his filet mignon. This was truly a world away from Carlucci's Ristorante.

Hoon spoke comfortably, as if we'd known each other for ages. "Work was crazy today. I couldn't break for lunch. Word that the Korea Development Bank was considering a buyout came just before First Watch. It was pandemonium when we closed up five percent. Jeez, Alice, I am so grateful you came back tonight."

He worked for a bank? What was I supposed to talk about? My IRA account?

"Don't let me shop talk, Alice. I can be pretty big bang about numbers. I don't want you to tell your friends about that boring guy you met last Watch."

Tell my friends at Carlucci's about my four star dinner with the handsomest man in two worlds while they dip their limp lettuce into bottled dressing? Not bloody likely. How could I share this with Peg? Or Ilene? It would be downright mean to tell Laura. Even if she marinated in Botox, she'd never look young enough for a hottie like Hoon.

Hoon mouthed something to our waitress. She returned with two warmed glasses of Sambuca topped with roasted coffee beans.

"I'm not a numbers person," I admitted. "But I'm not bored. I appreciate passion. What could be better than loving what you do?" I tasted the Sambuca. It was like everything else that night, warm and sweet. It was not the way I usually spent Tuesday evenings. It was so much better. Still, I knew a thing or two about life that I could share with him. I offered my caveat: "You should rest more and eat well. Even if you love work, don't give your life to a job."

Hoon raised his glass. "I want to work like a monster and love like a fool. So, when I'm old and dying, I'll have no regrets."

Is it really possible to die with no regrets?

"*Jah gi*, what do you do?" Hoon asked.

"*Jah gi?*"

"It's Korean for…friend," he hesitated.

"Really, so if I Google *jah gi*, Korean friend will come up?" My girl-radar knew he wasn't calling me friend.

"*Kul seh*, probably my dearest will come up. That's OK isn't it? We're going to be each other's dearest one day, unless you tell me something scary like you're into voodoo," he said with a laugh.

My dearest? I tried not to look at his full lips. What color would they be called? Tawny? Burgundy? I bet his nipples were perfect circles in that exact color. Oh my, what was I thinking? I needed to re-focus on his words. Just his words.

"You don't look like a big game hunter," Hoon teased. "I'm hoping you're not a mortician. Alice, you're not a taxidermist are you?"

Saying I stuffed dead pets for a living would be preferable to the truth. I can't tell him I earned my BA in English Literature with a concentration in Creative Writing only to end up a stay-at-home mommy.

"No, nothing like that." That stall would only buy me another five seconds. I need to use a career I know something about. What did I want to be since first grade? "I'm a writer," I lied.

"*Whah*, Alice, I'm impressed."

Oh, shoot. Now I had to embellish the whopper that just left my lips. "Basically, I was a ghost writer for several…companies…. But I'm not working at the moment," I wasn't sure when my mouth would stop. Luckily, Hoon jumped in. "You don't have to say it. They downsized, right?"

I nodded in agreement.

"What are you doing now?" he asked.

My brain went into overdrive. "I'm writing on my own…from home."

"*Chung mal?* You're the first author I've met. Maybe I've read you. What do you write? Mangas? Hypertext? Wikis?"

What the heck are mangas? I couldn't even remember the other two choices. Did he mean Kindle type things? Was it just Red Sky or had young people replaced all the universe's books with digital reading toys? "Actually, I'm working on a science fiction novel." What am I saying? Now I have to give details.

"That is so cool. Can you tell me what it's about?"

Why not. "Parallel universe travel," I dug deeper into my lie. If Hoon was a science fiction aficionado, I was dead. "This dinner is going to be expensive," I said, trying to change the subject. "Let's go Dutch."

"Let's go Korean tonight. My treat." He signaled our waitress. "Does your novel have a title yet?"

"*Blue Skies.*"

"Hmm. That's really good." Hoon signed the receipt and took back his card. We walked outside arm in arm.

He looked up at the burning sky. "*Blue Skies?* That's Wakie awesome."

It was. I had nearly forgotten the endless bright blue canopy of my childhood summers. Why had I been content to live out my days in black and white? Maybe I should write my story. Hadn't my college professors said writers get to invent their own endings? Me, in charge of the way my life turns out? That would be wakie-awesome.

Chapter

15: Staying Alive

Winter was dying hard. Another cold snap had studded the remaining snow mounds with frozen splinters. The TV news reported power outages on Staten Island and Brooklyn. I brought the laptop to the dining room table. It would be a good morning to stay in and start writing *Blue Skies*. Hoon had been so encouraging since I lied about being a novelist; my decision to actually write was more out of guilt than conviction. And I certainly had a tale to tell.

The drip drop of melting icicles as they clung in vain to the eaves, signaled it was time to stop for the day. I closed the laptop and massaged my tired eyes with my fingertips. Will was bringing Ruthie home that afternoon, but there was still time to enjoy a cup of coffee and remember my night in Red Sky.

Hoon had taken me to the Sony IMAX in Lincoln Square. We watched *Avatar* between swallows of Pepsi and sweetened kisses. Later, before my bus pulled away, Hoon pressed his palm on my window. I placed mine on the inside glass. For the last moments, even with a bus window between us, we were hand in hand.

The ringing house phone brought my reverie to a halt.

"I think something's wrong with my boiler," Laura began. "It's making funny noises."

Why call a plumber when your neighbor's husband could fix it for free? "I'll send Mike to look at it," I said for the umpteenth time over the years.

"Alice, you're a doll." She hung up before I could tell her that Will's Ruthie was visiting. I would call her later. No matter what, Laura had put up with my constant worries over Will. She'd love to hear my good news.

Mike came into the kitchen carrying dirty dishes and a half-empty box of chocolate doughnuts. He had returned to sleeping in the den again. I wondered what Hoon would have had for breakfast. My cheeks heated. I had no business contemplating Hoon's meals. I was married. My husband's standing right in front of me for heaven's sake.

Mike was decked out in a tan turtleneck and his favorite navy blazer. He even sported a pocket hanky. I wished I could have whistled to show my approval. I made a mental note to be more complimentary.

Wasn't that how we started dating? I had run into Mike on campus and told him his poli-sci presentation was the best in our class. He invited me to join him for a beer. Maybe I couldn't have cared less about his presentation but people like people who make them feel good about themselves.

"You look very handsome," I complimented.

"Yeah, but this jacket has seen better days," he plunked down his china and utensils on the counter. The clankety-clank of colliding fork and spoon jangled my nerves. "If you get over to Macy's, Alice, pick up another one. Forty-six regular. OK?" Mike took a toothpick from the cabinet.

He hated shopping. I bought all his clothes. Does he really think I don't know his size? "I'll catch their sale at the end of the week." I noticed his shined shoes. "You didn't have to dress up to meet Ruthie. Besides, they're not coming for hours."

"I promised Auntie I'd take her for brunch," he tossed his spent toothpick onto his plate. It darted the glop of leftover yolks and donut crumbs.

"Will you be able to eat after all that?" I pointed to the remains.

"I'll just have coffee." He readjusted his pocket hankie.

"I didn't know you were going out. I should have asked first, but Laura needs you to check her boiler." I headed for the phone. "I'll call her back and tell her you're busy."

"No problem. I can stop in at Laura's first." He took a Tic Tac box from his pocket and shook the last one into his mouth.

"But you'll ruin your clothes," I warned.

He tossed the empty box on his plate then walked past the trash bin on his way to the hall closet which made me think that Laura had the right idea. Just borrow a man for emergencies. Why clean someone else's dirty dishes every morning.

"I'll be fine." He straightened his collar at the hall mirror. "Keep Ruthie here if I run late. I want to check her out." He left through the front door. No kiss goodbye. No last hug. When love goes, it doesn't leave a trace.

I watched as he skidded down a patch of ice. He should have worn his boots.

It would be hours before Will's and Ruthie's arrival and the house needed a thorough shake out. Downstairs, the kitchen, living and dining rooms led into one another, making them a quick clean. Unfortunately, the boys' room had its original thick pile rug. I hauled the old Hoover from the closet. My house furnishings were Country French even though I had grown tired of the look by the time Luke and Will entered middle school. I preferred furniture with sleek modern lines but Mike was against re-decorating.

"Why would you throw out old junk just to replace it with new junk?" he asked me last year when I caught him duct-taping the bottom of the den's lounger.

So I wouldn't feel any more like Miss Havisham than I already do, I thought. That's why.

I vacuumed all the area rugs and carpeting then washed the kitchen and bathroom floors. After dusting and polishing, I pulled open the living room drapes to let in the sun and wonder what morning looked like in Red Sky.

A tableau of vintage figurines on the buffet caught my eye as if they hadn't been there for years. One by one, I removed the knick-knacks and put them into a drawer. I no longer enjoyed tag sale booty. Repurchasing mementos of my childhood had lost its appeal.

With my chores done and hair washed, I could think about my traveling in peace. I still didn't understand how I got there. Except for the Great Pretender, who would tell me? I can't ask Chrissy for the same reason I couldn't confide in Peg. They'll think I'm crazy.

I washed down my vitamins with more coffee.

There's always the internet.

After following several bizarre time-travel links, I stumbled on *The Grandfather Paradox*. It took me three readings before I got the gist of it: If I went to the past to kill my granddad when he was young, then I wouldn't have been born to grow into a person who could go back in time. That didn't apply to me. My body returned to its young state but I hadn't traveled through time. I traveled through place.

I typed in red sky.

"Aurora Borealis: From Aurora, the Goddess of Dawn.... Pollution, dust and water scatter red light causing the dawn sky to be red." I didn't care what the website said. Red Sky was not a polluted version of my world. It was the only place I could breathe.

Outside, a car horn honked three times. I looked out the window. Peg's Camry, with a crust of snow from the last storm still hugging its roof, pulled into my driveway.

I called from the kitchen door. "What a lovely surprise! Come in. I'll put up a fresh pot."

"The Tolans are not the kind who'd drop in unannounced!" She sneezed twice and cleared her throat. "Get your coat on and take a ride with me to the Book Nook. I know you're busy with Will, but I'm rushed for time today too, so I can get you back in an hour."

"Sure. Be out in a minute." I needed a real world distraction. Besides, bookstores were better than search engines.

I headed upstairs. My corduroys and sweaters were old and boring. It was much more fun dressing for Red Sky, but even if my night wardrobe expanded with me in daytime, I wouldn't have looked as good as I do in Red Sky. I pulled on my winter socks. I'll look like an old lady in these clothes. Maybe I should just stay home. I stepped into my cords. They zipped up without tugging. Are they loose? I turned in front of the mirror to check my rear. Not bad at all.

Peg wouldn't mind waiting another minute. I stripped down and weighed myself in the bathroom. Down five pounds? Traveling to Red Sky instead of night-binging on Haagen Dazs is way better than Weight Watchers. All right! I re-dressed and flew out the door.

무궁화

The Book Nook was as hushed as a library. I wandered through the aisles on my own while Peg placed an order for one of her classes. A display of Harry Potter books end-capped the aisle. What if JK Rowling didn't exist in Red Sky? Could I rewrite *Harry Potter and The Half Blood Prince* and become a billionaire in my alternate universe? Is Red Sky really an alternate universe? Or were the Great Pretender's words merely chatter within my dream? I put on my reading glasses, followed the signs to the science section and made my way towards the bottom shelves marked physics. My knees groaned as I squatted to read the spines. I couldn't even understand the titles. Peg was smart enough to decipher them but she'd ask about my sudden interest in quantum mechanics. I pulled out the closest book.

"Ma'am, would you like one of our mini benches?" A young sales assistant in the most startling black lip-gloss held out a plastic stepstool. I rose to my feet as swiftly as I could while speed-reading the back cover's largest font. "I'm trying to locate 'Tegmark's groundbreaking work concerning alternate universes,'" I said.

She took the book and flipped through the pages. Her ponytail swept over her shoulder as she pointed to a chart. "Is this what you want?"

It looked like a stack of colored pancakes. How could this teen-ager make heads or tails of it? Impressive. "Are you studying this at school?" I asked.

"Only if I went to Hogwarts." She snapped her chewing gum.

Wiseass. I peered over the tops of my readers. "Would you rather I asked your manager for help, dear?"

She quickly selected another book. "Here ma'am, you might prefer this one," she said. I skimmed the first paragraph: "Wave functions... probable states...quantum theory... separate but simultaneously existing...." This wasn't helping.

"I was thinking more along the lines of an account of someone who travelled to a simultaneously existing universe. Wouldn't they wonder about the unexplainable? How they entered or why their money was accepted there and how come things they bought there came back with them without a problem?" How crazy did I just sound?

The lip-gloss girl wasn't disconcerted at all. "You might find what you're looking for over in the Sci-fi section, but personally, I like my fantasies un-explainable. I know for sure that if you pound glass on a ballroom floor it will shatter, but I still believe Cinderella danced in those slippers," she quipped.

Out of the mouths of babes, I thought.

"Alice, do you want to stay a bit longer?" Peg called out as she headed my way. She had opened her coat and pulled off her hat. Static electricity lifted her wispy bangs till they stood at attention. I forced Tegmark's book back into the sales assistant's hands.

"Put your hat on." I told Peg. "You'll get sick." I rushed her out the door.

We sat in Peg's car facing a parade of shoppers. Most of the traffic was outside the hardware store. Sleepy faced men of all ages were lugging shovels and bags of salt back to their cars. Peg and I watched as if it was a drive-in movie. I suspected she had some-thing to share.

"I ran into Laura yesterday. I swear she gets younger looking every time I see her." Peg scowled.

"I know." I slipped my hand under my jacket to pinch my muffin top. It was definitely a half inch smaller. Maybe an inch. "Laura looks good since she trimmed down."

Peg pulled a clump of tissues from her coat pocket to block a sneeze.

"Bless you."

"Thanks." She slid the tissues between her wrist and her sleeve. "Weight loss doesn't remove wrinkles, Alice. Think like a girl. Didn't you notice her crows' feet had miraculously flown away?" Peg sniffed in.

"No…Laura would have told us. She's always going on about face lifts. We'd have to hear all the gory details if she actually had one," I checked my pockets for clean tissues..

"I didn't say she looked *that* good. I think she's had a few well-placed shots of Botox. But, jeez, she's crankier than ever!" Peg grumbled.

I remembered Laura's snarky comment when she saw Mike and me in our yard. I guessed I wasn't the only one who had noticed how ornery she'd become.

Our breaths steamed the windshield.

Peg flipped on the de-fogger. "It all started when I asked Ilene if she'd care to try the new Indian place for her birthday dinner. She was perfectly fine with it."

Why not? Ilene spent most of her mornings eating burnt Eggos with her granddaughter.

"So when I ran into Laura at the supermarket yesterday, I told her," Peg continued. "Alice, I swear she nearly bit my head off."

The forced hot air made me flush. My cheeks burned the way they did when Hoon whispered my name in the darkened theater last night. Hot nights were one thing, hot flashes were something else. I unbuttoned my jacket. "I'm guessing she didn't rush out to make reservations."

"You should have been there. She was apoplectic." Peg imitated our friend: "There's no parking lot. Indians eat weird shit. I'm not telling Ilene we're having goat curry on her birthday!"

I remembered my first taste of succulent grilled octopus the night Hoon and I ate at Dafni's after ice skating. I'd give goat curry a try.

"Anything's better than the same-old, same-old at Carlucci's," I said.

Peg took another swipe under her nose. "Amen to that. Laura wouldn't even give me a chance to tell her why I wanted to do something special. Ilene got more bad news last week."

"What news?" Why doesn't Peg just say it?

"Her husband's surgery didn't get all the cancer," Peg confided. "Nick's starting chemo next week."

"How terrible." My cousin Susan last year and now Ilene's Nick. Middle-age is not just the end of youth. Sometimes, it's the end.

Peg put the car in reverse and held back a sneeze. She was definitely fighting a cold. I hoped it was just a cold. When you pass sixty, every symptom is suspect.

"Buckle up, Alice." She edged her car out of the icy parking space. "It's like my sainted mother used to say…. Nobody leaves this world alive."

But I do, I thought as I handed Peg a fresh tissue. Nearly every night.

Chapter

16: The Book of Ruth

The chips and salsa were already on the table when I heard Will's voice outside the door. I watched through the window as a young woman in granny glasses and yards of ginger-red hair walked up the drive with him. She and Will were holding hands. This was a dream come true. Why wasn't Mike back yet?

They took their wet boots off at the door. "Ruthie," Will said as he awkwardly pointed at me, "this is my mother." It was exactly the way Luke had pointed to Emma when he brought her home on an earlier bright August day.

"Hello Mrs. Pleasance." Ruthie held out a box of chocolate covered doughnuts. "My mother said to give you these."

"Well, tell your mother these are my husband's favorites," I said. "Would you like to stay for dinner? We can have them for dessert." I led her to the kitchen.

"No." She surveyed the room. White porcelain bird and fish statuettes on the window sill stole her attention for a moment. "But thank you."

Ruthie had the fresh face of a high school student. Tall and slender, she carried her flowing silk shirt over her leggings with the stature of an egret and like Will, her youthful appearance belied her thirty-five years.

"I'm so glad to see you again, Ruthie. Come have some salsa and chips. I have sour cream dip too," I pulled out her chair.

Will piled a stack of corn chips onto a plate and handed it to Ruthie.

She folded her hands and said grace. I peeked to take in their bowed heads. Whatever their special needs took from them, it supplied them with life-long youth. To Him that brought us this wonderful moment—Amen!

Ruthie carefully chewed a chip then drank her soda before speaking. "Will took me to his veterinary clinic. I saw a sick beagle with respiratory problems. There are many breeds with respiratory problems but usually they are bull dogs. Pekinese have the most respiratory problems. They get them from over-breeding."

Ruthie's words tumbled out like blocks on a playroom floor. Her speech was marked by equal down strokes on each syllable indicating the same struggles with social language that Will had.

"That's why," Ruthie wiped the corner of her mouth with her napkin, "I don't watch dog shows. Even though my favorite breed is German Shepard, I think breeding is bad. Not as bad as what the poachers do in Africa…."

"Ruthie, TMI, too much information." Will instructed softly. I thought of all the times I had corrected him in the same patient tone.

Ruthie stopped to accept a chip dunked in salsa from him. "Yes," she agreed.

My lessons hadn't been in vain. Will had paid it forward by sharing them with his girlfriend. *My Will is a man with a woman by his side.*

"Your name is very beautiful," I said as I poured a second helping of soda into our glasses. "I've always liked the story of Ruth."

In the same way Will turned his head when meeting new people, Ruthie looked away from me when listening. I was sure Ruthie had been diagnosed with Asperger's Disorder too.

"It's from the Old Testament. Ruth was Naomi's daughter-in-law," she said. "We're a missionary family at Grace Covenant Church in Moshi." Her soft voice grew stronger as she spoke on a more familiar topic. "That's in Tanzania. We're going back in the springtime. My father told Will he should come too, so he can see the elephants and lions."

I wondered what Ruthie's father said to Will? Did he think Will could work with wild animals? In Africa? I hadn't considered Will living so far away. What if it was too much for him to take in? Then again, this might be the opportunity of his lifetime. I shouldn't get ahead of myself. It was just a visit.

Will took Ruthie on a guided tour of our house. They stopped at the den cabinet to dig out an old photo album. I re-dusted the hallway pictures to eavesdrop.

"Look Ruthie," Will pointed to a photo. "Here's our Halloween picture from second grade. Luke was Mighty Mouse, I was Mickey and you were Minnie. Luke found us sunglasses and told everyone we were the three blind mice. Remember?"

"I remember," she answered. "Luke put his mouse ears on Ginger."

Why had Mike and I avoided Luke's childhood pictures? Why did we bury the laughter? I tried Mike's cell. It rang from his night table. *Shit.*

Whenever Emma visited Luke, I had given them privacy. Will and Ruthie deserved the same. I busied myself in the laundry room.

"Mom, we're going," he called.

I ran upstairs balancing a stack of dryer-warm towels to say goodbye at the kitchen doorway. At the end of the drive, Will said something that made Ruthie lean into him and smile. He placed a kiss on the top of her head. I hoped they were still in the kissing stage. Did Will need the talk about sex again? Mike explained it all to the boys when they reached puberty. And I was pretty sure Luke kept filling Will in as they grew but that was years ago. Mike should call Will now before he and Ruthie go off alone. Maybe Mike hadn't left his aunt's yet. I phoned her place.

"Hi, Auntie."

"Alice, that girl who comes…. She's been stealing from me. What's her name?" Auntie's recent wild suspicions were another nasty symptom of her dementia.

"Joyce."

"Well, I just counted my spoons. I had service for twelve. Now, there's only four. Fire her, Alice. I don't need a darky cleaner who steals," the old woman commanded.

"She's not your cleaning woman, Auntie." *And please stop saying darky.* Her tongue was sharp as ever only now it included racial epithets. When I was growing up, people didn't think twice about using slurs. Even my mom. What would she have called Hoon?

Before my mother passed, she was the darling of her senior center's staff. The Guyanese kitchen ladies fawned over her. Yet I could almost hear her voice: "Alice, I have nothing against Orientals, but dating that Hoon boy? Really?"

Mike's aunt was getting impatient. "Speak up, Alice. You young people always mumble!" Auntie was thirty years my senior. To her I was still one of the young people.

"Joyce is your home health aide. Dr. Jason said she has to come every day. Anyway, why would she want your spoons? They're not silver," I tried using reason.

"Well, who knows? She could steal them and quit. She's transient."

Auntie couldn't remember my birthday or the last time she showered yet she could correctly use the word transient.

"But Auntie, she has a New York City license in health care. The police would find her. Is Joyce with you now?" I asked.

"Joyce? Is that the girl Luke's living with?"

Conversations with Auntie could sometimes circle the drain for hours. I had to pull the plug. "Is Mike still at your place? Put him on. I'll tell him about the spoon theft," I assured her.

"Was Mike supposed to come today?"

"Yes, Auntie. Mike took you out for brunch today. Is he on his way home?"

"I haven't seen Mike in nary a fortnight."

Fortnight? Auntie's dementia had returned her to her London childhood. I hung up to let her enjoy her past. I knew what it was like to escape to a happier place too.

Chapter

17: *Gweeshins* and *Gumihos* and *Mudangs*, Oh My

The Rapid Eastern Metro was late. I had been pacing to keep warm in the frigid March winds until I stopped to admire my gently-used Manolo Blahnik boots. The week before, I had braved a thunderstorm to shop at a Long Island estate sale for these suede beauties.

I had recently re-stocked my Red Sky wardrobe with clothes from both worlds. My denim minis with cotton blouses were replaced with tube skirts and asymmetrical cashmere tops. Why had I thumbed my nose at fashion all these years? Clothing is portable art work. How wakie-awesome was that! I spent my days scouring winter close-outs for designer bargains and last week, added Victoria's Secret to my retail outings.

Since my junior year at college, I had had only had two lovers. The first I met at a fraternity keg party and hadn't seen since. The other, I married. Neither made my body hum. I had feared even dreamy Hoon couldn't live up to the hype of a Barbara Cartland love scene.

But on St. Patrick's Day, Hoon's caresses ignited my libido like a Roman candle. Together, we fought through the parade crowds to make love like teenagers at his place. We hadn't planned having sex and neither of us had been cautious. That night, with a sea of emerald Erin Go Bragh flags waving below Hoon's terrace, we erotically baptized every room in his apartment. Hoon was a generous lover whose intensity never faltered. Even if there were ten thousand parallel universes, I knew I was the best-loved woman ever.

By the time the bus arrived, a half dozen of us clamored on board. I squeezed past a bony-kneed woman to claim the last empty window seat. One breath and I knew why she rode solo. My sallow-cheeked seat-mate reeked of marijuana. I bet my packets of magic seeds took me to a far better place than hers did.

As we approached the Queens Midtown Tunnel, I read Hoon's cell messages. Where r u? Where??

After Hoon and I became lovers, I went to Red Sky more often. Neither he nor I wanted time away from each other. On Friday, we began with long kisses in the elevator and continued till we lay in each other's arms under the tangled bed linens. He asked me to stay. I could only promise to be back next First Watch.

At 34th street, I wrote, "B there soon."

Hoon was waiting at the front of the queue. His handkerchief was folded into an intricate wave in his breast pocket as if he had been fitted by an English tailor but his tie was loosened after what was probably a busy Second Watch at work. I stepped off the bus and into his arms.

His lips brushed against my brow "I want to be with you, Alice," he murmured and added just as softly, "all the time."

"Me too." I meant it even if I didn't know how it could happen. I straightened his tie. "Are you hungry?"

"Not for food. Let's go back to my place," he beckoned.

Just like our first time, our delicious lovemaking was both adoring and fervent. When we parted last Watch, I worried the intoxication would fizzle. How wonderful to be wrong.

Hoon's bedroom was plain but not un-thoughtful. The Italian modern dresser and lowboy against the taupe walls worked well together. There were no dust-catching curtains but rather wide black lacquered blinds. It wasn't decorated enough to have been done by a professional or girlfriend. But it wasn't too manly for a woman to share. I liked his apartment from the heated bamboo flooring to the piquant leather fragrance of the new living room couch we picked out last month. The only frilly entry in his unfussy bedroom was a pink eyelet picture frame that featured teenaged Hoon holding a tennis trophy while his beaming mom looked on.

"Is this your mom?" I asked on my first visit.

"*Eung*, that's my *umma*, the formidable Mrs. Na," he said.

"Mrs. Na?"

"Na Moon-hee, my mom. Korean women keep their family names. My last name is Park. Actually, it's *Baek* in Korean, like my dad's," he explained.

No wonder I couldn't find Hoon's mom on the list of the dead that snowy morning. I was looking for Park. But then again, she wouldn't be on the list in my world. Or would she? It wasn't important. Right then, I was glad her picture didn't face Hoon's bed.

"Will you stay the night?" The back of his hand glided over my thigh.

"I'll have to get back," I said. We were ending our love-making with the same conversation again.

"Why?"

"It's not what you think."

Hoon had stretched out on his side to face me. "Good, because what I'm thinking sucks."

I snuggled into him.

"Another time," I purred. *Would that ever be true?*

"Next time, Cinderella. Promise. *Yak sok?*

"*Yak sok.*" We linked our pinkies Korean-style to seal the deal.

Even our afterglow was heady. We showered and dressed together in our new intimacy. Hoon set the kitchen island with an earthenware tea pot and poured two cups of Sothian green tea. We let them cool while we planned the evening.

"There's a *Men in Black* marathon in Soho," Hoon read from his iPad screen. "They're showing one, two and three. It doesn't end till Ten a.m.—First Watch but I'll drive you home."

I felt my palms dampen. It always scared me when he talked of going to my house.

"There'll be Watch-Change traffic on the Expressway. You won't get back before Second Watch," I said as I hopped off the stool and opened the cabinet above the sink. "Honey or sugar for your tea?"

Hoon tugged on my wrist. "*Ahn juh*, Alice. Sit down."

I returned to my seat like a schoolgirl.

"Do you live with your parents, Alice? Is that why you can't be late? Why don't we go back to your place so I can meet them?" Hoon flashed a smile at me. "I'm two years older than you. I have a job and no student loans. Asian is the new white. They'll like me. Besides, your folks would probably feel better about you coming to Midtown every First Watch if they knew a big strong guy was protecting you. *Mat chee?*"

My folks? Definitely not *mat chee*. That wasn't right at all.

"Alice, you're not answering," he was growing impatient with me.

The iPad burst into our conversation with the movie's inter-planetary battle scene. I put my hands over my ears. "Oh, that's so loud. How do I shut it down?" I was avoiding the conversation and Hoon knew it.

"Why don't you shut it down the same way you shut down every time I ask about your life?" he asked. "You know, when I dare to ask the none-of-my-business questions about where you live and who lives with you." He lowered the sound.

We sat in silence while Will Smith exterminated an alien on the small screen. It felt like an omen.

But it wasn't time for confessions. Not that I had any idea when the right time would present itself but I knew it wasn't then.

I blew on my tea before drinking. "I didn't want to tell you…"

Hoon leaned across the island to take my hands in his. "You can tell me anything, *chung mal*, really."

"I live in the Keebler tree with the elves," I said. "Like all wee people, they're a possessive lot so I can't bring you home just yet.

It's not as bad as it sounds. Snow White has it worse. The dwarves never keep cookies around."

He let me go. "I'm not laughing, Alice."

Even when I was alone in my day world, I couldn't bear to think of telling Hoon the truth. He'd see me as either a psycho or a space creature. Either way, I'd lose him. I wish he'd just appreciate our time together. I hurried to his side and put my arms around his neck. "Isn't it enough to know I'd rather die than hurt you," I tried reassuring him.

Hoon's phone announced a text. He ignored it. When it rang, I handed it to him and left for the living room.

"*Yeh*, Spenz." He covered the phone with his palm. "You were saved by the bell, *jah gi*. In future, if you want a cookie, only come to me. No more elves."

At least the tension between us was over, but how was I ever going to tell him about the real me?

Hoon and Spencer spoke in a sort of *Konglish*. Sentences began in one language and ended in another. This conversation was mostly Korean, but I could tell he wasn't keen on whatever Spencer was saying. "OK, Bro." Hoon looked at me to share his joke. "But I'm telling you she's not that kind of girl." Who isn't that kind of girl? Me?

He tossed the phone on the couch and beckoned me to sit beside him. "Spencer needs our help tonight. You can say no."

No to what? Is that kind of girl one who stays the night instead of disappearing like a ghost? What has that got to do with Spencer?

"Alice…. do you cook?" Hoon massaged the back of my hand with his thumb.

That kind of girl? Have we reached the comfort zone in our relationship? Was Hoon ready for a domestic arrangement? That must have been why he wanted to see my home. He's ready to meet my family. My family!

We'd eaten together, hung out with friends together, made crazy love and showered together. He was just making a normal assumption. Besides, I had to admit Hoon had always picked up the check for our dinners in Red Sky. But cooking for him and Spencer?

"What exactly…?"

"It won't be a big deal. Most of the food is pre-made," he said. "It's the third anniversary of Spencer's father's death. Koreans have to have a *ki-il*, the memorial for a deceased parent every year."

Hoon stood and faced me. "All right, I'll come clean. We need a woman to cook and set the table. That's how it's always been done."

I got up off the couch. "Let me get my tea." Maybe I should suggest take-out.

"We don't have much time. It has to be set up in the next two hours." He followed me. "It's *really* important to him."

Really? Then Spencer should have planned better. "Are you sure I should be the one doing this?"

"Please, Alice. Spencer's sister usually prepares everything but she's working a Watch Overlap." He put his hands together as if in prayer. "I'll be your BFF."

Why did he have to be so darn cute? It really wasn't a big deal. I'd been cooking for men since gasoline was 55 cents a gallon. Another meal wouldn't kill me.

"So this is a regular memorial service?" I asked. A pot of coffee, a couple of pound cakes and a few prayers, how different could a Korean memorial be? "It's just a little something to honor his dad, right?"

"*Kul seh.*"

"What does that mean? You know I'm Christian. I don't want to do anything to dishonor Spencer's beliefs," I said. Mostly, I didn't want to break the first commandment. "It doesn't involve spirit worship does it?"

"Well, there'll be the usual small and large animal sacrifices and later the *gu mi ho* foxes will drop their tails," he kidded.

"OK, you've paid back my elf joke but don't tease the cook. Your next bout with food poisoning is in my hands." I made jazz-hands for emphasis. "Seriously, it's just a regular memorial service, right?"

"*Eung*. But the *gwee shins*…they'll fly through the windows."

Why did that sound so scary? What flies at night? Bats? Witches? What was I getting into, Korean Halloween?

Chapter

18: The Duty of the Living

Spencer's kitchen was a narrow galley that could comfortably hold two cooks who worked in perfect harmony. Unfortunately, that wasn't Spencer and me. We stood shoulder to shoulder frying dumplings and making very small talk. We had spent a lot of time together and while I enjoyed Spencer's company, the truth was I thought of him as *Hoon Light*. He was clever and funny and almost as handsome as Hoon. But Spencer was a player. Even though he had a girlfriend, his eyes strayed whenever a pretty girl passed him on the street.

I squeezed past Spencer to get more oil. "Jeez, Alice," he complained. "You're drowning the *mandoo* in sesame oil. And what's up with the *ddeok*?"

"Do you mean this?" I pointed to a filled tray that looked like a solid sheet of rice pudding powdered with cinnamon. "I thought you said to slice the *ddoek*."

"Not like that!"

I was about to tell him where he could shove his *ddeok* when Hoon stepped in for a minute and did it for me in Korean.

I placed four more frozen dumplings into a less oily pan. "Is Hyun Soo coming soon?" Hyun Soo was Spencer's latest who rarely joined in our conversations and habitually applied several coats of lotion to her hands throughout our meals.

"I can't ask Hyun Soo to help," Spencer said. "She's Korean." He took the last of the produce out of a bag. "My father's *ki-il* service will eventually be prepared by my wife. If I ask Hyun Soo, she'll think that's the direction we're headed."

"I understand." I understood all right. Lotion-loving Hyun Soo was getting cut from team Spencer.

"Shit." Spencer searched though the emptied grocery bags. "Alice, did you see the *Cheong ju*?"

"Is that the big tan apple-looking thing?" I wasn't a fan of being laughed at but my ignorance seemed to lighten Spencer's mood.

"No, Little Euro, *Cheong ju* is rice wine," he patted my cheek.

We could hear Hoon pushing Spencer's couch across the living room. "*Hyung*," Spencer shouted, "Did you bring *Cheong ju*?"

"I'm going now. Everything's up and ready when you are," Hoon called back.

We finally began working in tandem and even managed a congenial rhythm. I held a small wooden pedestal while Spencer topped it with cooled fried *mandoo*. "My sister's much better at this than I am," he admitted while we finished our preparations. "She knows the proper order. But I know white's the traditional color of mourning. It's why there's white *mandoo*, white *ddeok* and the peeled *bae*. That's the apple-looking-fruit. The *Cheong ju* is rice wine. It's clear like water but don't let it fool you. It kicks like a mule."

"Your guests eat only white foods?" I asked.

"This food isn't for guests. It's for my father's spirit," Spencer clarified.

"So what we prepared was an offering? But Hoon said something would fly out the windows," I said.

"The *gwee shins*. They're ghosts. Don't worry. Hoon was kidding. I don't believe in random spirits," Spencer filled a metal bowl with rice. "But I admit I believe my father watches over me." He stopped to wipe his hands on my apron as if we had been grade-school friends. "Did Hoon tell you I called you a *gu mi ho* after we first met?" He flashed a very Hoon-like smile.

"A fox?"

"A nine-tailed fox who seduces men." He stuck a pair of metal chopsticks into the rice. "I thought you were too good to be real."

"And now?"

"Now, I envy Hoon. I wish I could have introduced my dad to the woman I loved," his cheeks reddened.

Hoon told Spencer he loved me? I should pay more attention tonight. In case Hoon asks me to make his parents *ki-il* services.

"Spencer, on the anniversaries of Hoon's parents' deaths, does he prepare all this by himself?" I asked.

"No. Hoon's folks were Christians like my Mom. They wouldn't allow a memorial." He dried another pedestal with a paper towel. "I'll show you my Dad's picture," he said as he tossed the towel into the trash.

He returned with a photograph trimmed in a black and white striped ribbon. It showed a friendly faced Korean man who looked my real age. Except that now I wasn't sure what my real age was. I felt more real as young Alice.

"He was handsome." I put my hand on Spencer's arm. "I'm sorry you lost him so young."

"Me too. He took this picture right before his bypass surgery. I guess he knew it would be his memorial photo. The week before he died, he told my sister and me, 'Life's a long road. It's the duty of the dead to leave the path and the duty of the living to keep walking,'" he ran his hand over his father's photo.

I had tried to keep walking after my son's death but I had only managed to drag myself through the years. Luke would have hated my defection from life.

I untied Spencer's sister's apron and realized how far I had come. I had truly released the hideous past without losing one precious memory of my son. Making peace with Luke's passing had finally led me back to my path. *Or was I on a new path?*

I folded the apron carefully before returning it to the countertop. Even though I was ready to begin again, how could I sort out my two lives? I really had to think seriously about this. What was that famous St. Augustine quote? Sed noli modo. But not just yet.

"Grab those two white bowls, Alice. Let's see if your boyfriend remembered how to be Korean." Spencer led me out of the kitchen.

Hoon had transformed Spencer's living room from a millennial man-cave to a devotional temple. The couch had been set back to accommodate a white paper screen. The tufted leather hassocks were replaced with a low mahogany table. Spencer and I nodded our approval as we carried in the prepared food. Together we set a row of pedestals and a row of bowls on the table. Spencer made room in the center for the photo. As he instructed, I lit the slender white candles.

"Should I light the incense too?" I asked.

"No, I'll do it later."

Just as we had finished, Hoon returned with a bottle of *Cheong ju,* and helped me tidy the kitchen. "These things are not gender friendly." Hoon whispered, "Usually, Spencer's sister stood at the back of the room. But you'll be able to see the whole ceremony from there."

"That's OK."

Spencer met us in the kitchen in a fresh shirt and tie, "*Hyung,* are you and Alice ready?"

"We're ready." Hoon put his arm around his childhood friend. "Are you?"

"As I'll ever be. Let's do this." We entered the living room together. I took my place in the back.

Spencer lit the incense with a white candle, presented a bowl of *Cheong ju* to his father's picture and took a few steps backwards. His slim legs tucked under his torso till his whole body folded. His palms went flat on a flowered silk floor mat when he touched his forehead to the wooden floor. He brought himself up like a fish breaking through water and bowed again.

Hoon made his double bow with the ease of a gymnast. When he rose, Spencer joined him in a standing bow.

Spencer's father smiled his approval from his place of honor.

Chapter

19: The Best of Men

I balanced my purse, three grocery bags and a jug of orange juice, and still managed to shut my car door with my hip.

"Need a hand?" Jeanette Novak shouted from across the street. She was strapping her son's bike onto her car rack while her youngest child wailed in his stroller.

"You have your hands full already. Besides, this is my weekly weight training," I shouted over the passing cars.

"Good one, Alice," she shouted back.

I toddled like a storybook milkmaid from my car to the side steps.

The unmistakable odor of burnt bacon met me at the kitchen door. Mike had scorched a half pound of Hormel trying to make a BLT sandwich. I opened the kitchen window and turned on the exhaust fan.

"I told you I'd be back at one," I said. The blackened grease sizzled as it poured down the drain. "I'll make your lunch." I peeled three slices of bacon from the wrapper and heated the cleaned pan.

Mike added the rest of the package to the skillet. "Alice, don't fill the sandwich with lettuce like you always do. Real men eat meat," he shook his finger at me.

While I drained the slices on paper towels, Mike snuck a slice of buttered bread into the pan. "Let the extra fat soak in," he watched the steam rise off the slice.

"What are you aiming for? Suicide by cholesterol?" I removed the greasy bread from the pan. "Your cardiologist warned you about your blood results."

"Dr. O'Hara is an Irishman. He knows the importance of a perfectly poured pint and pork fat. I'm taking my Zocor, so don't be a nag," Mike shot back.

Nag? Did I ever complain about the crap he left for me to clean every time he had a snack? "I'm trying to help you live longer. Who knows…we might be visiting our son in Africa someday. We'll want to be fit enough to make the trip," I said with a smile.

We had talked about Africa several times since Will declared himself. Mike wasn't keen on it.

He leaned over the counter and wrapped his beefy hands around his sandwich. Were his hands that chunky when we were young? Hoon had long tapered fingers with clean straight cut nails.

"I'm sure Ruthie's enough of a handful for her parents," he said. A toast crumb shot from his mouth. "They probably weren't seriously offering mission work to Will. They were just being polite."

"I hope not. Think about it. Our Will has the opportunity to care for animals he's only seen in zoos." I massaged Mike's shoulder. We'd disagreed about what was best for Will since his diagnosis, but I knew Mike loved him as much as I did. "How about we invite Ruthie's parents to dinner? We'll see what kind of people they are."

"Dinner with missionaries! Jesus, why couldn't Will find a normal girl?" Mike chomped down another bite. "What's so funny?"

"You said normal. The Coles are probably asking the same thing about Will." I handed him a napkin. "Our Will's the best. I'm sure Ruthie's parents know what a great guy he is. Besides, there's a bonus to all this."

"Is that supposed to be funny too?"

I had learned to tread carefully when speaking of Will's future. I changed the conversation to something I thought we'd agree on.

"Well, if Will serves in a mission family, he'll be funded by the church. Then his 9/11 compensation money can keep growing. We can rest in peace knowing Will is financially safe. He could even…," I didn't get to finish.

"He could even what?" Mike nearly bit my head off. "Be a big shot investor? Besides, that victim's compensation money was given to us! It was your idea to save all of it for Will. Luke would have wanted us to…. What's the use of talking about this again?" He took the last of his sandwich up to the den.

Us? Like we'd ever enjoy money that was given for Luke's death? Would a yacht replace our first born son? Could Mike actually enjoy driving a Porsche that was paid for with Luke's blood?

I filled the sink with the frying pan and dishes. Why shouldn't Will have it all? Mike and I weren't going to live forever. The fund money was the nest egg for Will's future. I gathered up the utensils. The spatula slipped from my grasp and fell. Bacon fat spattered the floor. I hated getting stuck with all the chores. I hated the tired kitchen with its worn linoleum tiles and faded country French valences over the blinds. Most of all, I hated being married to Mike. I bent down to lob the greasy spatula into the sink.

Its splash down left bacon fat circles floating on the water. They reminded me of when Will worked at Wal-Mart. That rainy spring, when our Luke had been gone five years, Mike was still determined to remake Will into his brother's image. After work, he'd have Will play one-on-one basketball for hours, trying to convince him he'd play as well as Luke with practice. The dad who loved Will when he was Luke's twin now constantly compared him to a ghost who couldn't be beaten.

Will buckled under the pressure. He picked at invisible scabs on his face. He started to stutter. His counseling visits grew from once a month to twice a week. His meds were tweaked and re-tweaked.

One evening, the schoolyard drains backed up coating the basketball court with oil-slicked rain water. Most of the neighborhood boys had abandoned their games but Mike had insisted Will practice after his shift. Dinner grew cold and the sky darkened but Will and Mike hadn't returned from their game. I drove to the court to find Will covered in perspiration and hopping from leg to leg.

"Do you have to go to the bathroom?" I asked. "I'll drive you home."

"Let him try again." Mike's face was flushed and damp, but he threw another lay-up.

"How many tries so far?" I asked.

"Not that many. Let him try."

"It's thirty seven, Mom," Will battled his frustration. "I missed thirty six times. I need a restroom."

"Get in the car."

Mike didn't ride home with us. For weeks, I tried to reason with him.

"Will is not Luke. You have to let Will be Will."

"He can't be. What's he going to do?"

"He's really good with animals. Maybe he can work at a pet shop."

"My son is not going to be a dog cage cleaner!" Mike shouted inches from my face.

I had heard all I needed to hear. By that autumn, I had signed the papers to place Will in the Ladders Group Home. Within three weeks, he stopped picking at his skin. After a month, he no longer stuttered. He started training at a veterinary clinic and made two new friends. Mike and I fought bitterly over my decision. Often our arguments lasted late into the night. We went for counseling.

The psychologist suggested our shouting matches weren't about Will. He said it was our way of mourning Luke. We didn't make another appointment. Over the years, Mike and I still had our verbal skirmishes like the one that just played out but this one struck deeper.

I put the groceries away; ketchup in the cabinet, chicken breasts in the freezer, toilet tissue under the bathroom sink. I was glad nothing required actual thought. I refrigerated the mayonnaise and rinsed the cutting board. There were no more little chores to keep me from screaming. I had to get out of that house.

I grabbed my coat off the back of the kitchen chair. Will deserved his place in the world and he wouldn't have been able to claim it if I hadn't sent him to Ladders. Thanks to Mike's outburst, I remembered exactly why I had to make the torturous decision to send my surviving son away. I slammed the door behind me.

Chapter

20: Small Pleasures

I joined Ilene and Peg for Ilene's birthday dinner at Carlucci's. Was the décor always this drab or was it only in comparison to the eateries Hoon selected? I had just taken off my coat when Ilene ordered a bottle of house red for the table.

"Laura said she'd be late tonight. We can start without her," Ilene said downing her first glass right after it was poured. She put on her bifocals and pretended to study the same menu we had been reading for years. Nick's chemotherapy had begun earlier that week. If it were my husband, I would have cancelled our dinner, but Ilene was the most agreeable woman I'd ever known. Like Peg's joke telling, Ilene's pleasantness enhanced our dinners. Of course she hadn't balked at Peg's Indian food suggestion—she would have agreed to chicken eyes in blood sauce if that was what the rest of us craved. She was the perfect balance to Laura's recent moodiness. I couldn't say the same for myself.

"Would you be interested in taking a course at Adelphi this spring?" Peg attempted to engage Ilene. "The Continuing Ed department is offering Pottery, French for beginners and a writers' workshop."

Ilene didn't look up from her menu. "Maybe some other time."

Peg turned to me. "You should sign up for the workshop. It would get you back in the swing of writing. Besides, I bet you'd be the only published writer in the class."

"Peg…"

Ilene looked up from her menu. "You should write again, Alice. You were good at it."

"A short piece on collecting mid-century cocktail shakers for the local newspaper doesn't make me a published author," I protested.

"You wrote it and it was published." Peg wasn't dropping the subject. "What about all those short stories you wrote in college? Didn't you win something in your senior year? The DeLorean something?"

"The Lorian Hemingway Short Story Competition," I corrected her.

Peg knew perfectly well what I had won. She tricked me into saying it aloud.

"That was forty years ago," I hastened to add.

"So what? A published author is a published author," Peg turned to our friend for backup. But Ilene had already buried her nose in the entrée section.

"That reminds me," Peg said as she tapped on Ilene's hand to recapture her interest. "Ilene, do you remember Eve and Burt Cutler? They were my neighbors."

"The art teachers?" Ilene asked

"That's them," Peg answered. "I ran into Eve at the bank. She's divorced and coming back to Queens. We started talking about the old days and the holiday parties she and Burt used to host." Peg nudged me under the table. "Ilene, did you ever see Eve's Christmas tree?"

Ilene slid her glasses onto her head and listened.

"Eve hand-painted all her decorations," Peg told us. "Her Christmas balls were works of art—delicate snowflakes, cute puppies in red bows. She's really talented. Anyway, I asked if she still had them. She said Burt gave them to his mistress. Well, you know what that means don't you?"

By then, Ilene and I hung on Peg's every word. "First that slut took Burt's *balls*. Then she took Eve's!" Peg lifted her wine glass. "OK, ladies, raise your glasses. To Eve, and all the other women who have lost their balls."

Ilene put down her glass and rummaged through her quilted tote till she fished out a matching billfold. "Speaking of Christmas, did I ever show you Caulder's pictures with Santa?" She pulled a photo from its sleeve. "Other kids on the line were crying but she went right to him." She flipped to another picture. "My son took this one last week. Look how big she got in just three months."

She was trying to rally. Good for her. I wished she had been with me the night Spencer talked about his dad. No matter what happens, Ilene, keep walking on your path.

We had finished our salads and most of the wine by the time Laura entered the dining room. Collectively, yet without a word between us, we hid our reactions to her mid-thigh sweater, curly new coif and black metallic tights, but Peg couldn't contain herself for long. "Mutton dressed like lamb," she remarked sotto voce.

Laura waved a gift bag, barely missing a busboy's tray. "Ilene, wait till you see my present. Nick will ravish you tonight!" she squealed.

Had we forgotten to tell Laura about Nick's chemo? She wouldn't have mentioned Nick if she knew. Would she?

Ilene put away Caulder's pictures and sipped her water as Laura re-capped how she chose the perfect style and color for her hairdo. Eventually Laura ended her story with a slurp of wine. It had gotten awkward. Peg would have had to pull a rabbit out of a hat or read our palms to liven the mood. By the time the waiter returned to take our entrée orders, we were drinking in silence.

"My usual," Laura spoke first.

"Me too," Ilene added.

"What's the chef's best dish?" I asked the waiter.

He looked up from his pad. "The chef's special is a Bronzini in lemon and garlic that's to die for. Get it with pilaf to soak up the sauce."

Laura broke off a chunk of bread from the basket. "Don't you know what a rip-off the chef's special is?" she said. "That's how restaurants get rid of their old fish before they reek."

The waiter said something in Italian to the busboy filling Laura's water glass. He signaled back by rolling his eyes.

I wondered why Laura was still in my life. I couldn't remember when we had fun together. My friends in Red Sky knew how to have fun. Peg and I have fun. Even Mike occasionally was fun. It isn't like having fun is hard. Couldn't Laura have helped make Ilene's birthday dinner a fun time?

I let my feelings fly. "Laura, I know what a rip-off *life* is, but I don't stop breathing when it stinks. Let's just celebrate the moment."

Ilene lifted her glass. "Here, here."

"I'll have the Bronzini," I announced before polishing off my wine.

"Waiter, I'm changing my order." Ilene put her napkin on the table and stood up. "I'd like a penne in vodka sauce…and a bottle of Chianti for the table." She unhooked her tote from the back of her chair. "Would you all excuse me, I'm going to the ladies room to take off my Spanx."

Whether Ilene's new bravado was from three glasses of house red or my own burst of boldness, it sure felt good to bring down the curtain on our ennui.

무궁화

By the time I returned home from dinner, the cobalt sky had deepened to charcoal. I stood in the driveway watching a lone cloud nuzzle the moon. When was the last time I had seen a crisp night sky over my driveway? Usually, the red-blue mist blurred all sights and sounds up until the end of my street. But that, of course, was only on Red Sky nights.

My phone signaled a text. *Hoon?* No. My phone worked perfectly in both worlds, but never inter-universally. I checked the screen. It was a message framed in quotation marks from Ilene. *Thank you for letting me be myself.* I texted back, *My pleasure!* I wondered if Hoon also had dinner with friends. Where had he eaten lunch? Why couldn't I spend my days with Hoon too? Mike wouldn't miss me. The last day we spent time together was our snowball fight.

"Mom."

"Will?"

Will held open the side door. The kitchen light outlined his broad shoulders. I scrambled up the steps to greet him.

"Are you and Dad having a boys' night in?" I asked.

"We went for burgers. Dad's asleep now. I got a pass to stay here tonight. That's OK, right?"

I kissed his cheek. "That's great."

Often, on chilly afternoons after school, Will, Luke and I sat at the kitchen table dunking marshmallows in hot cocoa till they disappeared in our cups. The boys vied for fastest dissolver but more important to me was hearing the events of their day.

Will rested his elbows on the kitchen counter while I heated milk for our cocoa, just as he did when he was little. Like his brother and father, he had a high forehead but his soft blonde hair and pale blue eyes were all mine.

"Sweetie, would you get the marshmallows?" I asked. "They're in the cabinet over the micro. And get the Nillas too." I wanted to ask him about Ruthie and her family. "Let's sit at the table." I set our cups next to each other. "I think Ruthie's even prettier than when she went to Higher and Higher Academy with you."

Will pushed his marshmallow down to the bottom of his cup with his spoon. "No. Ruthie was pretty then too. Now she's taller and bigger."

"Does Ruthie miss Africa?" I shook out a handful of vanilla wafers from the box. "Is that why she's going back…soon?"

He lifted the spoon and watched his marshmallow rise to the top of the cup, "I want to go to Africa so I can see elephants. I asked Ruthie's father if I could do mission work in Africa. He said as long as I was baptized in a Bible-believing church, I could start training. But even if I can't be part of the Moshi Ministry, I'm still going to marry Ruthie. I love her and she loves me."

My son in a ministry of service? Maybe, but handling the trials of marriage? Does he like Ruthie that much? I needed something a lot stronger than cocoa to wrap my head around this.

"Will, you haven't seen Ruthie in a long time. You and she should date for a while, like Luke and Emma did," I brought Luke into the conversation for support.

"Luke and Emma didn't date that long," he salvoed back. "They moved in together after a year. Luke told me—don't move in with a woman until you really know her. Ruthie and I know each other since elementary school."

I took a long loving look at my grown son. He had the same right to fall in love as anyone. But dating was one thing. Getting married was something else.

"You haven't seen Ruthie since you were eighteen," I pointed out.

"Ruthie and I were pen pals after she moved away. And when Luke died, we friended each other on Facebook," he countered.

Why hadn't I kept up with Will's social life? I didn't even know he posted on Facebook.

"Will, marriage is a big step and going to Africa is a major move." Was I advising my son not to follow his dreams? Shouldn't everyone be allowed his dreams? What about me? Should I stop dreaming? "Sweetie, sometimes things other than love make you want to take chances. Are you sure what you feel is love?"

"Mom, I'm happy with Ruthie, even when she doesn't let me kiss her," Will made his point.

I was happy with Hoon even before we moved on to kissing.

"I like to hold her hand and tell her stuff I think about," he continued.

Whenever Hoon held my hand, I wanted to tell him everything in my heart.

"I like to listen to her talk about Africa."

And listen to Hoon talk about Red Sky.

"I like the way she smells."

God, how I loved breathing in Hoon's cologne.

"That's how I know I love Ruthie."

That was how I knew Will loved Ruthie.

And how I knew I loved Hoon.

Chapter

21: April Love

Somewhere between March's leonine entry and lamb-like exit, Hoon and I entered the comfortable second stage of lovers. No longer an occasional traveler, I spent every First Watch with Hoon. Our dates evolved into breezy decisions made sitting side-by-side on the couch. Mostly we went to dinner, made love and rested in each other's arms. Occasionally, Hoon drifted off. I couldn't allow myself to join him.

Hoon's doorman greeted us with his usual affable smile. "What do you think Miss Alice? Are these April showers gonna bring us flowers?"

"I don't know, Bill." I tugged my hood from my hair. "It's pretty rainy."

"Well, it may be rainy but you're the one who's pretty. You call me any time this man is mean to you." I couldn't imagine a mean Hoon.

"Bill, how come you're so friendly towards Alice?" Hoon teased. "Everybody else gets, 'Have a good Watch.'"

"Everybody else ain't Miss Alice," the doorman said. "There's nothing better for a man than a young woman with an old head. Young is just a loan. Maturity pays dividends forever." The lobby concierge seconded Bill's words with a nod.

"Wait right here. I'll get your mail." Bill headed for the rows of numbered brass mail boxes.

Hoon impatiently tapped his finger on the handle of his umbrella while we waited. Earlier, we had rushed dinner with friends to get back to his apartment alone. And it wasn't to pick up his mail. Bill returned with two envelopes and walked us to the elevator. "Have a good Watch."

I adjusted the collar of Hoon's trench coat as our elevator sounded a tone for an approaching floor. Hoon pretended to preen in the security mirror. "*Gam sah.* Now my collar's impeccable. What would I do without you?" he asked.

"Let's not find out." I longed to have an honest relationship with Hoon. I was sick of the constant pretenses. But if he found out I'm a much older woman with a boring middle-class life behind me, what would he do? He couldn't love the real me. Could he? Hoon had already questioned my comings and goings. Surely he'll ask some in-depth doozies when I come clean. Somehow, I had to explain my nomadic metamorphosis even if I haven't figured it out myself.

He lifted the straps of my tote from my shoulder, "I don't know how you lug this around all Watch," he said. In one swift move, he transferred my bag onto his shoulder. "Only a manly man could get away with holding a girlie bag," he said with a wink. I adored this man and I needed him to love me back, internal wrinkles and all.

Maybe *Mudang* Kim had returned from his Korean pilgrimage. So what? He'll probably just talk rings around me and offer more seeds. Why hadn't he explained anything? Perhaps *Mudang* Kim isn't a very good *mudang*.

Hoon's phone buzzed a text. "It's Spenz. He wants to hang with us. Don't worry he won't get past Bill. I'll text back *no*, just in case. I want us alone till next Watch," he said.

I slipped my arm through his. Me too, me too.

Hadn't the Great Pretender questioned why my *mudang* didn't give me any information? Realistically, as if anything in my life could be called real, the Great Pretender was a better source for information. How could I track him down in a city with thousands of bars? Unless Vintage is his local, the Great Pretender won't be easy to find. Even if I do, why should he stop partying to help me?

"Hey, earth to Alice from the moon." Hoon planted a kiss on my nose. "You were so lost in thought. You didn't answer me. Have you memorized the new door code yet?"

"112935." We are so definitely a couple.

"*Khrum*. Yes, but did you figure out the meaning?" His smile was downright magnetic.

"You're grinning, so it has something to do with me," I guessed. "Is it a date? Like 11-29, November twenty-ninth? Is thirty-five for nineteen thirty-five? Is it something I should remember?"

"Alice, why would you need to remember 1935?" he asked.

It was the year my mother emigrated from England.

"Dang." Hoon opened the belt on his trench coat and checked his inside pockets. "I think I left my office USB in my car. We'll have to head down to the parking lot for a minute."

The parking lot! The Great Pretender said he owned the parking lot near Vintage. He'll probably be there most First Watches. I'd have to concoct a story to leave Hoon's place early. But if he insists on walking me to my bus stop, then what?

"I'll give you until we reach the sub-basement to crack the door code. Need a hint?" Hoon placed a wayward strand of my hair behind my ear. It was all my heart needed to flutter. Maybe I'll put the Great Pretender on hold for one more night. Then again, he might just know how to keep Hoon and me together in Red Sky.

"Let's see…no hints just yet," I said. "You know I'm not a math whiz so you wouldn't have picked an obscure equation. I'll guess the numbers stand for letters. Am I right?"

"*Whah*, Alice. Beautiful and smart."

I began calculating on my fingers. "The eleventh letter in the alphabet is K."

"Cold. Keep trying."

"What do I win if I guess?"

He caressed my neck.

"Don't distract me," I wriggled from his hold. "I think I've got it. The first number isn't eleven, is it? It's one. It's A! Then twelve is L. You entered my name." My prize was a long luscious kiss.

More than anything, I wanted to play elevator kissy-games with the Hoon who loved the real Alice. I'd have to find out how I got here and tell him the truth. What if Hoon leaves me? I drew in a long breath. Whatever I have to do for him to genuinely love me is worth the risk. I had to find the Great Pretender even if it took a thousand and one First Watches.

무궁화

We walked through the damp parking lot aisles with our arms wrapped around each other. When Hoon reached into his car, I began casually.

"I'll have to leave a little earlier tonight," I said. "I'm trying to meet with this expert on companion universe travel. He's been lecturing in New York on the distinct universes within the multi-verse theory that are parallel universes." I was overdoing it. "It's for *Blue Skies.*"

"*Oh di?* Where's his office?" Hoon closed the car door. "I'll take you there."

We had spent the long winter Watches revealing our inner work-ings to one another. I knew he wasn't just offering a lift. But there was no getting out now. Besides, isn't there a word for lying for a very good reason? Yes, answered my conscience, it's called lying.

"I don't think he has an office. He's kind of eccentric," I said. "There's a bar called Vintage in the East Fifties that's his usual haunt. I'll just pop in on my way home."

Hoon's eyes widened. "No problem. I'll go with you." We headed back to the elevators. "Alice, I don't know what things are like in your secret neighborhood, but it's dangerous in Manhattan."

My girl-radar blipped. Hoon was really wondering how danger-ous I am.

"You'll need a tough, *kum do* expert body guard when you meet up with some science fiction guy in a singles bar. *Guk jung ha ji ma,*" he said. "Don't worry. I'll stay with you. When you're done, we'll pick up ice cream and pig out back here. Isn't that a better plan, *jah gi?*"

He's not thinking about ice-cream. And why would he? I disappeared and reappeared with no discernible roots or connections. But was I ready to bring together Hoon and the man who knew my real age and heaven only knew what else? What if the Great Pretender told Hoon about our daytime lives? I better start praying that Hoon won't believe such a crazy story until he hears it from me.

We reached the elevator bank. "You're not saying we should go now?" Hoon asked.

"After," I assured him. "Definitely not now."

"Then I'll have to make *now* last a long, long time."

"Absolutely." I let my fingertip remain on the up arrow.

Chapter

22: I've Changed Several Times Since Then

The rain had long stopped by the time we left the apartment, but the street drains had only managed to corral the puddles into a slippery basin under the curb. Hoon held my hand as I crossed over. It was my first step towards telling him the truth.

Except for the addition of a fizzled Tiki torch, Vintage's oak and brass entrance was as I remembered it. Inside, paper-maché masks and blow-up palm trees lined the walls. A sign proclaiming *free drinks for hula girls* hung from the ceiling. As we tried to get through the crowd, a bartender decked out in plastic leis called out, "Welcome to Luau Night. What can I get you?" We pretended not to hear him. I continued through the revelers with Hoon close behind. Out of the crowd, a hand cupped my bottom. In a second, it was smacked off by an irate Hoon. "Alice, is this expert worth getting pawed?" he demanded.

"If he isn't at the bar, we'll leave," I promised. Then what will I do?

The Great Pretender was in an orchid Hawaiian shirt and perched on the same stool as when we first met. This time he was singing to a red-head who was checking her texts.

"Excuse me," I said. The scent of peaches tickled my nose. "Do you remember me?" He had to. How many women in Red

Sky smelled like peaches? What if there were hundreds? The darn seeds should have made us telepathic too. Then I could have sent him my thoughts—this is on the sly, the QT, the down-low. Capice?

He tossed a fifty on the bar. "Goodbye Mona Lisa. It's been real," he said to his red-head. In a flash, he was off the barstool and kissing my hand. "I could never forget you. I knew we'd hook up eventually."

Hoon stepped in to make his presence felt. I steeled myself for Armageddon. I had to say something fast.

"Hoon, this…is the world's leading authority on parallel universes," I stuttered through my terrible introduction. "This is my boyfriend, Hoon Park." That sounded even worse.

The Great Pretender raised his eyebrows in my direction. Had he caught on? Would he play along?

"Nice to meet you, Hoon." The Great Pretender and Hoon managed a handshake in the crush.

Behind Hoon's back, I clasped my hands together under my chin as if begging. "Would you answer a few questions for my research?" I asked.

"Anything for the sake of research," he said. Good, he'll play along.

He raised his voice above the din. "This place gets too damn crowded on theme nights. Why don't we talk, you know, where we had our last Q and A?"

Outside, he flicked his cigarette to the curb and asked us to follow him.

Unlike my first night in that parking lot, there was a constant flow of cars. A car jockey in a red jacket handed off keys to a customer then headed in our direction. The Great Pretender waved him away. "We're OK, Alfonso. Just talking to my colleagues."

I took out my cell phone and hit my Evernote app. It wasn't likely I'd forget anything I'd learn about my travels, but it didn't hurt to take notes for *Blue Skies*.

I saw Hoon size up my parallel universe expert. My man knew me well enough not to be jealous over this one. "I'll wait over there," he pointed towards a bench at the lot's kiosk.

The Great Pretender spoke as soon as Hoon began walking away. "You know the rules, Alice," he cautioned. "If you fall down the rabbit hole, you're likely to get stuck."

I hadn't told him my name. How did…? Oh, he meant *Alice in Wonderland*. Well, that was a fair comparison.

"I really appreciate this," I said. "I won't keep you long."

"The last time we met you were in a hurry too. So why'd you come back? Care to explain yourself?" His thick eyebrows inched closer together like storm clouds.

"I can't explain myself because I'm not myself," I said. "There was a time when I knew who I was but I've changed so much since then."

He patted his pockets till he found his cigarette pack. "The seeds'll do that."

"I want to know why I'm in Red Sky. How did you get here? Where exactly are we?" I asked.

"Whoa! Did you just call this place Red Sky? I think of it as Second Life but that's as good a name as any." He leaned against a graffiti-covered van and took a cigarette. "So what do you call yourself?"

"I'm Alice Seaton."

"That's as good a name as any, too. My real name is Joseph De Noto." He took a business card from his shirt pocket and handed it to me. "Most people call me Uncle Joey. I think I already told you I started coming here in 1989. Back then, one of my companies manufactured stainless steel throttle pedals. You probably see my trucks every day. Big red logo? Pedal Pushers?"

I slid his card into my purse. He owned Pedal Pushers? That's a huge corporation.

"Anyway, I was in Pohang South Korea signing a multi-billion dollar contract. I turned fifty-five with a shit load of money," he sucked on his cigarette.

Lucky him. When I was fifty-five, I was mourning Luke and paying off Will's medical bills.

"See, I missed out on the partying other guys got. I was stuck in…doesn't matter. I didn't want to be a geezer barfly handing out twenties for feels. Let's face it, even if I got hair plugs and major nips and tucks, my insides would still be five decades old and counting. I wanted a whole lot more," he exhaled his smoke for punctuation.

A white convertible sped onto the lot knocking over a traffic cone and spilling out a glassy-eyed rat and his dinner. The driver, a slender black man in a pork-pie hat, shouted above the engine noise. "Hoon! My brother from a paler mother is that you?" He raced to the bench to bear-hug Hoon.

Thank goodness, a distraction. We had more time.

The Great Pretender restarted our conversation. "One night in Seoul, a gorgeous *ki saeng*, that's means geisha in Korean, anyway, she tells me her uncle is a famous *shaman* named Jeon, who…"

"Why aren't there more of us?" I interrupted. "It's easy enough to get the seeds."

"There could be more of us," he said. "For all I know, all the milk carton kids live here. Why didn't you ask your *mudang* when he sold you the seeds? Anyways, for the right money, Jeon said he'd bring me to a guy who could really make me young. Right down to my DNA."

What was the right money? For as long as I knew Laura, she hadn't spent more than twenty dollars on a gift. I made a dollar sign and a question mark on my screen.

Joseph looked over at Hoon. "Your boyfriend is telling his buddy about you. That's one happy bastard."

I didn't turn around. Could I keep Hoon happy? I crashed into his life with no thought of how it would end. He deserved a Red Sky woman, not me in a mask.

"You've stayed unattached, Joseph. Perhaps, I should too. I think Hoon would be better off with a girl his own age," I didn't mean a word of it.

"Maybe, but that's not what you feel, is it? Tell the truth. Would you stay if he begged?" Joseph asked.

"I'd stay if he said don't go." But would that happen once he knew the real me?

Twin clouds shook out their last few raindrops before passing on. Joseph held out his hand to feel the air. "I hate the damp, but all that red and blue mist at the entryway is pretty cool, isn't it?"

"Entryway?"

"You had to notice the fog that meets you at night."

"Yes. Of course, the purple droplets that wait outside for us," I said. "And once we're through it, we're here."

"Smart girl." He crushed his half spent cigarette under his heel. "Like I was saying, next thing I knew, I'm meeting this Taoist *mudang* who called himself Mr. Kim. Who would have thought it, a Korean named Kim. Heh!"

"My *mudang's* name is Mr. Kim, too. Is he the reason I keep meeting Asians in Red Sky?" I asked.

The rat twitched its whiskers and sped off in our direction, veering off just inches from us. I hopped backwards, dropping my phone. Joseph picked it up.

"Who knows? I've got my own theories about our travels. I think the seeds find us. Between you and me, I had a lousy youth. Doesn't matter why. Anyways, now I can be the life of my own party." He wiped down my phone with his handkerchief. "I know that Koreans are big on settling debts. Did one of your ancestors make a promise a long time ago?"

"How could I have a Korean ancestor?" I twirled a lock of my blonde hair.

He handed back my phone. "Then maybe the seeds are the path to your Asian soul mate." Joseph pointed his chin in Hoon's direction. "Besides, this is New York City, baby. There are probably millions of our Eastern brothers and sisters here."

"If this is also New York, why did you first tell me the universes weren't identical?"

"Because they're fraternal," Joseph explained. "Most things are the same, the Statue of Liberty, Golden Gate Bridge, the Super Bowl, stuff like that."

"Are most people the same too?" What would I say if I ran into Peg? Good heavens, what would she say to me?

"I was told some people are the same, but from what I've seen, people live either here or there. The old me isn't here and neither is the old you."

"How do you know I'm not already here?"

"Come on, you've had plenty of time to track down your family," Joseph shook his head. "And don't tell me you never looked."

The first thing I did was search for Luke. "You're right. I haven't found my…relative."

"That's the point. This world and our world aren't exactly the same," he said. "So if your *relative* can't be found, it's because your family doesn't exist here, never did. That includes you. Get it?"

Got it. Will and I didn't have alter-egos in Red Sky. And Luke died only once. Somehow, that was comforting.

Joseph snapped his fingers in front of my face. "Alice, I don't have all night. Why don't you ask me something important, like why we're twenty-six?" He looked over my shoulder again to check on Hoon. "It's because after age twenty-six, the eye and brain cells that signal each other start to die."

I wrote "cell signal" with three exclamation marks, then added a question mark. "So, everyone who takes the seeds becomes twenty-six again to allow the eye and brain cells to communicate?"

"Uh, oh. Don't turn around. Your boyfriend is watching us. Let me make this fast," Joseph said. "Do you know what Magic Eye puzzles are? Kids play with them. You stare at what looks like a jumble of flat images and then suddenly a 3D picture jumps out at you. Well, that's what this place is. It's always there but we can't see it. The seeds signal our eyes and brain to create a mega-stereopsis."

I added "mega-stereopsis" to my notes. "Is it the signals that let us see inside the puzzle?"

"Yup, but they don't work for everyone. There are people whose lines of vision don't intersect the right way. I forgot what it's called." He tapped his finger on his lips. "Sounds like the violin. Stradivarius, maybe?

"Strabismus?" I scribbled "Laura has Strabismus." as fast as I could.

"Yeah, that's it. Anyway, they can't see 3D images so they can't enter what you call Red Sky," he said. "As far as I know, they're the only ones who can't."

Maybe Laura bought the seeds for herself and when they didn't work, she re-gifted. But that wouldn't explain why she bought them in the first place. "What would happen if a Red Sky person came to our world?" I asked.

"Don't even think it, Alice. I was advised not to try to bring anyone back. And it didn't sound like a *suggestion*," he warned.

It wasn't important. I'd never ask Hoon to age forty years for me.

"Alice, are you sure your *mudang* didn't go over this when he sold you the seeds?"

I hadn't met *Mudang* Kim till I already had the packets. "My friend Laura bought them for me."

Joseph smirked. "What woman gives away eternal youth?"

"It was my birthday present."

"That still doesn't make sense. Why wouldn't she take them? Unless the seeds didn't work for her," he offered.

Now I knew Laura lied about seeing Luke in her dream.

"She gave me the seeds for my insomnia," I said. It sounded preposterous when said out loud.

I heard Hoon say goodbye to his friend. "Is he coming this way?" I asked Joseph.

"He's about to. I take it you don't want him to know about your first life," he said.

"Did you ever tell anyone, Joseph?"

"Like who? The women I meet on barstools? You and I should meet up in our world. My address is on my card. Know where Douglas Manor is?" he asked.

"Yes, I'm in Floral Park."

"No shit? We're practically neighbors."

I had to admit, Joseph was growing on me.

"So Alice, since we're fellow travelers and fellow Queensites, tell me, is that your real name?" he asked.

"Well, I'm not *the* Alice but things are certainly curiouser and curiouser in Red Sky," I answered.

Joseph took in the sky above us. "Maybe I'll start calling this place Red Sky too." He lit a new cigarette and blew out a perfect smoke ring. "I'm heading back to the luau but I'll leave you with a little present."

Joseph made a megaphone with his hands. "Hey, Park, this woman loves you too much. She's supposed to concentrate on her writing but all she does is talk about you."

Hoon's face beamed as he walked towards us.

23: The House of the Lord

After a lifetime of attending Sunday services at St. Andrew Presbyterian Church, including years of worship with my twins in tow, I arrived alone on Easter for the first time. Will had gone to Grace Church with Ruthie. Mike, who rarely came to church, had stopped completely after my last birthday. I greeted my friends in Praise Team and stopped to listen to ancient Mr. Clunes complain about his prostate.

Why had I worn this flowery Easter hat? Last night I was Boho chic when Hoon and I met Spencer and his latest for a karaoke throw down, yet here I am bobbing up and down through the pews with a garden party on my head. I can imagine the church gossip: Did you see poor Alice Pleasance all by herself at services and in the most hideous hat!

The usual songs of praise were followed by the reading of *Hebrews 11:1* and church news. Only during the sermon was I able to fill my heart with the Gospel. I took my communion grape juice and bit of unleavened bread back to my seat to pray: Father God, I've been to Red Sky twenty three nights in a row. I'm guessing all this traveling displeases you. Even so, please don't let anything weird happen to my body or my soul.

What kind of prayer was that? I paused to wait for a thunderous downpour of fiery brimstone. When I felt safe from God's wrath, I continued. Forgive me, Father, I've been a terrible sinner but really Lord, I'd been mulling this over for weeks. Didn't you send Laura with the seeds?

A howl went through the hushed sanctuary. Not heavenly condemnation but only a fussing infant in the back row. I apologized to my maker.

Lord, just give me wisdom and patience. I know Luke is safe from suffering in your eternal home so as always, I lift up my son Will for your protection. And since you're the Lord of all, could you please watch over Hoon Park too?

As one body, the congregation stood to raise its hands and eyes for the benediction. On cue, the side doors opened. St Andrew was not a pretty church. Built in the 1950s, it was a mélange of fake slate and ultra-modern fixtures but it was where I first heard the Word. It may have looked more like the Explorer space mission than house of God but it taught me not to judge a book by its cover.

The after-service collation in the social hall was meager since most of the parishioners had left early for family dinners. I stood next to a tray of glazed donuts and crullers while nodding back to the dwindling number of familiar faces.

"Alice, it's providential to see you blocking the sweets," a voice resonated behind me. "Yesterday, I pilfered a bag of jelly beans from my daughter's Easter basket. The spirit is willing, but...." Pastor Morgan was an ample Scotsman with a voracious appetite for Jesus and junk food. Neither could be hidden since his conversations were filled with both. I liked everything about him from his sonorous pronouncements to his beautiful mind. More than that, I trusted his opinion.

"Thanks so much for today's sermon, Pastor," I said. "It's good to be reminded that what is seen is not made of visible things."

"Yes, the assurance of things hoped for never fails to stir the heart," he said. "But don't thank me, I'm just the messenger."

He selected a napkin from the stack next to the sugary crullers. "Gluttony always starts innocently, like picking up a calorie-free napkin." He put it back.

"I was hoping to talk to you this week," I said while fidgeting with the brim of my hat. I should have taken it off after services. How much credibility do I have with this drooping rose in the middle of my forehead? "When may I stop by, Pastor?"

"How much time would you like?" he asked. I doubted he realized he ran his finger through the excess powdered sugar on the tray and licked it clean. He was definitely the right man to discuss temptation.

"Not very long. It's just a short question about…pleasing the Lord," I assured him.

"No time like the present. But let's steer me away from this table. I can walk you to your car. Is this too important for a parking lot, Alice?"

I answered with a non-committal smile.

We managed to weave through the fellowship stragglers and slip out the side door. I spoke over the crunch of our footsteps on gravel.

"I've decided to…actually, I'm taking a creative writing course and I've written a character that may be dabbling in," I hesitated. "Well, you see, she essentially goes to an alternate universe."

I had just lied to Pastor Morgan. On the day of my Savior's resurrection, I was attempting to manipulate my pastor until he gave me the answer I wanted. No wonder I go to Red Sky. It's the closest I'll get to heaven.

"I see. Well, Alice, maybe we should set a date to meet," his tone grew serious.

Why did I start with such a ridiculous opening? It's too late now. I can't say, never mind Pastor Morgan. Go have a cruller. I pressed on.

"What if a character, a Christian, told her pastor that after she goes to sleep at night she wakes up thirty-six years younger in another universe?" I asked. "At first she enjoyed visiting, but then she wanted to stay, to begin again. Don't get me wrong, she knows a second chance doesn't guarantee a better life, but still, hypothetically, what would her pastor say?"

A driver waved from his SUV as he exited the lot. Pastor Morgan called out a greeting then rubbed his chin with his knuckle. "Pastors are privy to so much of life's challenges. I hope, truthfully I pray, that whenever one of our church members has a heavy heart, she'll be comfortable talking about it with me, anytime. But we're only talking hypothetically. That's what you said, right?"

Busted. Pastor Morgan deals in troubled souls for a living. Of course he saw right through me. Maybe I should have just laid it all out. Pastor, I need Hoon and Red Sky but I also need to know I'll still be right with God.

As if he had been waiting for my internal conflict to make up its mind, he kept silent till we reached my car.

"So, Alice, a short story is it? Good for you. I like the idea. Let me think. I know pastors who would say she was possessed. They'd get her exorcized. Is that where you want to take this tale?" he asked.

"No." Definitely not.

"Perhaps this is more about changing one's life. Back in seminary, we used to say 'born again' but maybe you mean a renewal, a reboot," he raised his eyebrows in question.

Reboot? Like a computer? Could I just press stop and start again? Would my memories stay with me like my laptop's Favorites bar?

"Are you saying she could start again in another universe?"

"I don't see why not. We're all broken, Alice," his eyes sparkled while he spoke on his favorite subject. "Our Father's amazing grace is given freely, not earned like a scout badge. Wherever you take your character, she will dwell in the house of the Lord forever."

Amen to that.

Chapter

24: A Walk in the Park

I had nearly finished wrapping the last of my creamer collection for the church White Elephant sale. The year after Luke died, I filled the kitchen with vintage glassware—dozens of aqua flowered water glasses and nearly as many orange juicers. The following year, I amassed a collection of mid-century pitchers I'd never used. Last spring, it was creamers. I didn't need a shrink or Pastor Morgan to tell me I was trying to fill the gaping hole in my heart with stuff. It was time to de-clutter. Like all living things, I needed room to grow. I taped the ends of the tissue paper and hoped whoever bought the Arzberg creamer would see its elegance despite its damaged spout.

The house phone rang.

"Alice, it's Peg. What are you doing right now?"

"Spring cleaning, but I'd love a break. What's up?"

"I need to start jogging. I figured we could meet up on 260th Street and jog to the Glen Oaks Oval, do a few laps till we're tired or paramedics have to resuscitate me, whichever comes first. What do you say?"

I'd say, somebody call out the bugle corps. The last time Peg Tolan exercised was to squeeze into a dress for her niece's wedding. And if I remember correctly, the niece recently delivered her third child.

"Should I stop in at Laura's and ask her if she wants to come too?" I asked. Why was I still including Laura in my plans?

There was a significant silence until Peg broke it with an imitation of our friend. "Laura? As in *I'm not so vain that I'd go under the knife for my strabismus?* Besides, Ol' Lazy-Eye Laura will just trip over her feet as usual. We could end up in a three-lady pile up. Wouldn't want that." Peg snickered at her own joke.

I didn't defend Laura. "I'll be there in five."

Mike was at the kitchen table filling in the newspaper's crossword puzzle.

"I'm going out with Peg," I said.

"When are you coming back?"

Where was the husbandly, take care, see you later, buh-bye? He probably only asked when I was due back so he'd know whether he had to make his own lunch.

"I don't know. Possibly, not till the cows come home," I answered in disgust.

"OK." He didn't look up.

무궁화

In her black crew neck and yellow jogging suit, Peg looked like a cartoon bumble bee exiting her daughter's Volvo. Trish, Peg's youngest, got out of the car to greet me. At twenty-five, she could have easily been my besty in Red Sky.

"Trish, I so love your hair band."

Trish's long black hair and big hoop earrings reminded me how much I missed Chrissy. She was due back from China soon. I couldn't wait to see her reaction when I tell her about Hoon.

I kissed Peg's daughter on both cheeks.

"You are too cool, Mrs. Pleasance," she said. Trish handed me her velvet band for a closer look. "They have amazing designer ones at Loehmann's. Try to get my Mom to go with you." She pointed to Peg's faded fanny pack. "Maybe she'll be inspired."

"Your mother is already the most inspiring woman I know," I said.

Peg gave me a thumbs-up while hugging her daughter goodbye.

"When was the last time you jogged?" I asked as Trish drove off.

"I think I forced myself to do it on my fifty-fifth birthday. That was almost ten years ago," she admitted. "That means I jog every decade, whether I need to or not."

"I envy your determination," I said. "I want to be just like you when I grow up."

"And I, my sweet friend, want to be just like you if I grow down. And for the record, you're only two years younger. If you're nice, I'll tell what happens when you turn sixty four," she said.

A naughty joke was coming. "Tell me."

"Your hair turns silver."

"That's no big deal. I've had gray hair for years."

"I'm not talking about the hair on your head." Peg raised her eyebrows.

"Peg!"

We fell into a soft stroll around the Glen Oaks Ball Field. The ground, still soaked from a night's rain, suckled our heels. New mown grass perfumed the air turning a pleasant afternoon with a friend into a treasured memory. I hadn't welcomed a new season in a long time. "I'm glad you invited me. Nature's announcement of spring shouldn't go unnoticed," I breathed in the new growth.

"Save the poetry. You're wondering why I asked you to walk with me." Peg pulled at her dampened collar. "I thought it'd be cooler today. Then again, at my age I'm always enjoying my own private heat wave."

"Did you need something?" I asked. Instantly, I thought of Ilene's Nick. Peg wasn't going to tell me something awful, was she?

"Take it easy. Nothing's wrong. I've just been noticing your metamorphosis. At Ilene's dinner, you were like the Alice I met thirty years ago; feisty, confident. Hell, you're even dressing better these days." Peg caught me eyeing her bee outfit. "Judge not. I keep up with Vogue at the beauty parlor." She took a tissue from her sleeve and daubed the sweat under her bangs. "If we were bending our elbows at a pub right now instead of walking in circles, I'd toast your decision to be you again."

Was that what Pastor Morgan meant by rebooting; the decision to be me again?

"You're my muse, Alice," Peg continued. "You're why I'm out walking."

I stopped to look into her Irish green eyes. For years, I wished I was Peg—the perfect blend of smart and sassy. Why hadn't I noticed she was human, overweight and slightly disheveled, with a house filled with books that hadn't seen a dust cloth in decades? It was a lesson well learned. I needed a friend, not an idol. Peg was a wonderful friend. Could I share Red Sky with her?

"I was…."

She stopped me. "I have a favor to ask. How about planning my birthday dinner next month?"

My Red Sky moment had passed.

"You'll be in charge, Alice. Choose a time, date and a brand new place."

The last party I planned was Mike's sixtieth. We argued over the guest list. He added new names and crossed others off on an hourly basis. After I finally mailed the invitations, he insisted I un-invite Auntie. That's when I swore off party planning. "I'm not a party planner," I wasn't giving in.

"Maybe the old Alice wasn't, but the new Alice is. Actually, you're more like Alice, again; better, bolder but still you. *This* Alice can certainly plan a little party." Peg pushed on her elbow for a stretch. "In fact, don't make it little. I want it to surpass Ilene's party. Make it the best birthday I ever had."

Who knew? My friend Peg, mother of three and holder of two master's degrees had her heart set on being the special birthday girl. Even so, I needed to gracefully bow out of this.

"But, Peg…."

"It's not just that. I've been choking down Carlucci's high and dry salmon for years and all I got was this." She slapped the top of her butt cheek. "You know why? Because when I get home from our dinners, I pop the lid off Chef Boyardee's Ravioli and eat it with my fingers."

How many post-Carlucci dinners had I spent eating cold left-over mashed potatoes by the light of the refrigerator? I'd never guessed we'd bond over binge-eating.

"Alice, when you worked your magic at Ilene's dinner, I gave Chef B the night off," she said. We stopped walking for a moment so she could shake a pebble from her sneaker. "I swear one more dinner at the place where Italian elephants go to die and I'll take a steak knife to Mr. Carlucci. Come on. This'll be your birthday present for me."

"Did you have a theme in mind? Spaghetti-Os and the Modern Woman?" I joked.

"Try harder." She handed me a mini water bottle from her pack. "Something that heralds my healthy new life."

I twisted the cap. It wasn't sealed. I kept the bottle in my hands. Peg noticed. "And that's the first thing I'll do when Trish graduates and moves out. No more refilling my water bottles from the tap to save money. Maybe I'll even buy a fancy brand. I'll be liberated when she's done."

"Are children ever done?" I doubted her claim.

"Hell yes. We're supposed to raise them till they function on their own. Ergo, my kids and your Will are done," she insisted.

"Peg, you're very sweet but Will…"

"But Will my ass! He's a grown man. He lives at his own place. He's got a job with medical coverage," she left no room for discussion.

"Actually, he and Ruthie Cole…. It's serious." It felt good to brag about Will.

"There you go. You'll probably be a mother-in-law before I am."

Though we only sauntered around the bases, we stopped to sit in the dugout.

"Alice, the finest thing you did for Will was getting him into Ladders," Peg said. "You successfully pushed him out of your nest and into his own. Will's best days are ahead of him and so are yours."

Will, yes. But me starting again in Red Sky? However young I was there, I still had over sixty years of memories stored in my brain. Could I still have a tabula rasa ahead of me?

A young couple with a stroller and toddler in tow crossed the ball field in front of us. The dad took a blue plastic bat from his knapsack while the little boy's mom tossed a ball in his direction. Peg and I watched as the trio played out a familiar scene.

I took a mouthful from Peg's water bottle and sat back to enjoy a momentary daydream of Hoon and I playing with our children.

"Don't you envy them, Peg? Beginnings are wonderful," I said, stretching my arms high overhead.

"New beginnings. Is that my party theme?"

"Absolutely!"

무궁화

I returned home to find the leftovers of Mike's snacks sprawled over the kitchen counter. How could one man leave behind so much garbage?

"Mike, you home?" I waited in the stillness.

How hard was it to put things in the sink? It's not like we hadn't had this conversation a million times. Why'd he leave a coffee mug and a tea cup? Couldn't he have just rinsed and re-used? And what was up with the Lipton's tea box? I tossed out the empty jam tart box and his crumpled napkins. Washing the spoons and cups would have to wait. I longed for a hot shower.

As the steamed heat filled the stall, I began to plan Peg's sixty-fifth.

Elegant or fun? Fun, definitely. Peg's story about a hotel maid in Paris chasing her onto the tour bus with the panties she left drying on the balcony still made me laugh.

I had turned the knob too far and wriggled like a snake under the hot spray till it reset.

A coffee mug and a tea cup. When was the last time Mike drank tea? Does he have a sore throat?

The scent of my Vanilla shampoo reminded me of fresh baked pastries.

Maybe I can make a French bistro party. Maybe not. The closest I ever got to France was French fries and reading *Madeline* to the boys.

I rinsed the last of the shampoo from my hair and shut the tap. Something wasn't right.

The kitchen door squeaked open.

"Mike, is that you?"

No reply. Was he losing his hearing? I called out again. "Mike?" Why wasn't he answering?

I opened the shower curtain and caught the tap-tap of shoes on the kitchen floor.

Oh my God, it's the Glen Oaks robber. And he knows I'm here! I looked around the stall for a weapon—soap, shampoo, loofa and razor. I want to maim the bastard not lather him up and shave him. What if I turn the faucet to its hottest mark and point the shower head towards the door? If he came in, I could scald him.

I was at the ready, armed with my shower-hose plan, when I heard voices. There were two of them! I couldn't fight off a pair of robbers. Father God, get me out of here alive.

Someone rapped on the bathroom door.

"Alice, you back so soon?"

"I'm in the shower, Mike. Who's here?" I called through the door.

"I didn't know you were home. Laura just came by. She wanted to borrow one of your exercise tapes," he over-explained. "You said you were going out for the day."

I don't have exercise tapes. A hot flash kindled in my belly and raged to the top of my head.

A coffee mug and a tea cup.

Sweat and shower water dripped onto my feet. The thumping in my chest spread till it pounded at my temples.

Since when did Laura exercise?

I didn't even know anyone who still had a VCR.

But I knew who drank Lipton's.

"Be out in a minute," I could barely get the words out.

I closed the lid on the toilet seat and sat with my head between my knees. *Connect the dots. Connect the dots.* I had to stop shaking to think this out.

My wet bottom mingled with the moisture on the toilet lid forming a vacuum seal. I heard the kitchen faucet run and the cabinet doors creak. I visualized Mike wiping away the evidence. For once in his life, he was cleaning up.

I didn't do anything wrong. Why was I hiding?

It was only after I towel dried, combed the tangles from my hair and wrapped myself in my robe that I was able to face Mike. I found him tying up the kitchen trash bag.

"Didn't mean to hurry you out of the shower. Everything all right?" His gaze never left his loops and knots.

No, Mike, everything is not all right. My head is exploding. I want to punch you a thousand times and go next door to beat the crap out of Laura. "Everything's fine," I said calmly. "Why?"

"No reason, no reason. I was…Auntie called. The home health aide didn't show up. I'd better check on her. I'll take the trash out on my way," he stammered.

The door closed behind him with a swish and two clicks.

Pretending nothing had happened was a walk in the park compared to confronting him. While young Alice had no problem expressing her emotions in Red Sky, the older model was better at compartmentalizing feelings than unpacking them.

I brewed a full pot of coffee. While it was still hot, I poured all of it down the drain. I took the mug and cup Mike had just washed, wrapped them in a dish towel and hammered them with a rolling pin till my wrist ached, then shook out the shards into the bottom of the new trash bag and buried the rubble under an avalanche of steaming black grounds.

Chapter

25: Bruce Lee and Blondie

April nights, even under a red sky, are nippy. I pulled the lapels of my jacket up around my neck while pacing at the kiosk. By the time a Rapid Eastern Metro finally pulled up, I was shivering. I stepped onto the bus and headed for the nearest heating vent. My chills had nothing to do with the weather. This was usually my time to slough off other world worries before meeting up with Hoon but I had taken the local in error. The constant side street stops allowed me too much time to recap my day.

Mike had returned at dinner time complaining about the rush hour traffic on the Expressway as if he had really visited Auntie. I set down two plates of chicken croquettes, poured two diet Cokes, and dressed our salads at the table. We spoke about the broken windowpane on the garage door. By the end of our meal, Mike seemed pleased with himself, practically chipper.

He wiped his napkin across his mouth and crumpled it into a ball before chucking it onto his plate. "Can't beat a good croquette. It was just like my mum's. Moist on the inside, crunchy on the out-side," he patted his stomach.

Stuck in traffic on the way home from Auntie's? As lies go, it wasn't even a good one. How long has he been lying to me? Exactly when did he start spewing those wife-fooling whoppers to my face? I should have figured it out years ago. Why did it have to be on a day when I was happy? And why did I have to be naked in the bathroom suctioned to the God-damned toilet seat! I leaned my head on the bus window and closed my eyes. I didn't want to think about it.

We came to another stop. A gaggle of teens from Queen of Martyrs High School boarded. Even with their earbuds pressed deep into their heads, I could hear their music. I shut my eyes again as if it could keep out their racket.

Mike and Laura must have started fooling around right after Luke's death. That's when Mike went celibate. Only he wasn't celibate. Not with Laura.

The bus exited the Midtown Tunnel and headed uptown. My heart began its usual Thirty-Fourth street flutter. I could finally put my horrible day on the back burner.

Slow down little heart, we'll be with Hoon in a few minutes. Immediately my bubble burst with my own revelation. I was a cheater too.

I heard my mother's voice as clear as a bell—*Thou shall not commit adultery.*

Technically Mom, I argued in my mind, I'm not married in Red Sky. That kind of reasoning would have sent her into a tizzy.

Besides, Hoon and I…we're really in love.

That kind of reasoning was probably the same as Mike's.

The driver double-tapped his breaks. "Last stop!" he bellowed. The bus jerked forward and rocked back. I stood and reached for the pole. Why had Mike stayed married to me?

I made my way down the aisle. And why the heck did I stay with Mike? My chills returned along with a wrenching gut. Dealing with all this was making me sick.

Hoon met me at the bottom step. "Do you think you could leave your cell on?" he said. It was not a question.

"Did you try to reach me?"

"I gave up trying to reach you, Alice. You're not reachable."

Not tonight. I couldn't handle any more. Why was Hoon making a big deal about my not answering my phone?

"OK, so you couldn't talk to me for a few hours." No more drama, please. "I always come right after First Watch begins. No matter what my day is like." And, trust me, I just had the crappiest day ever. "You don't have a clue…. You have no idea what it takes for me to be with you."

He reached for my arm. I pulled it away.

Homebound commuters began taking an interest in our argument. A middle-aged woman tipped her readers down to get a better view, as if we were street performers.

Hoon's hand brushed mine. Just for a moment but long enough to keep me from a melt-down. I let him lead me away from the bus stop.

We walked in silence until we approached the next Watch Zone. The street grew quieter and traffic was thinning. At the corner of Third Avenue and East Sixty-Fourth Street, the Change of Watch warning lights flashed. Winkie the Bear reminded all to lower their voices before entering. Hoon and I headed for the pedestrian ledge in front of an office building.

"Alice, you're right. I don't have a clue, but neither do you," he chided me. "You're totally blind to what you mean to me." He wiped the city soot from the ledge with his hand before offering me a seat. "Meeting you changed everything. I still can't believe I have someone who worries when I work too hard."

Of course I worried. Sometimes he returned to his office after seeing me off.

"I walk around smiling," he grinned. "I pet stray dogs…I even wave back to babies in strollers. Last week, I started whistling to myself. Whistling! It's like I've never been happy till you."

That's how I feel.

"I want to wake up with you in the morning not sleepless all night wondering why you keep this mysterious schedule. I'm scared you'll disappear," he lowered his head.

I don't want to leave you, Hoon.

"I swear I feel like I've been waiting for you my whole life," he went on. "The night you found me buzzed on the curb, I was drowning. You rescued me."

I rescued him? Where is this conversation going? It wasn't as if I hadn't known he cared for me, but this was different. This was a major declaration. I let him talk it out.

"I thought I'd go crazy when you didn't answer my texts. I tried your WATCH GPS but it kept blinking 'failed'," he showed me his phone.

Did he mean the little blue WGPS at the bottom of the screen? Is that why it only came on when I was in Red Sky?

"Were you trying to track me?" I asked. Not that he could.

Hoon ran his hand through his hair in frustration. "Did you not catch the news? Lehman Brothers is bankrupt. I'm unemployed."

I had forgotten he worked at Lehman. Wait a minute. They went belly-up two years ago. What do I say without sounding like a fortuneteller?

"Didn't this… already…."

"Didn't I see this coming? *Yeh*, the night the Korea Development Bank pulled out, I pumped up my resume and packed up my office stash of ramen cups. Goodbye dream job," he waved his hand.

"Oh, Hoon, trust me there'll be better job. There always is." I patted my shoulder in invitation.

He rested his head in the crook of my neck.

"I'm ashamed of how greedy I am, Alice," he revealed. "I have no job, but I still have to have you."

"No worries. You had me at, *Ahn yo ha seh yo*," I assured him.

"Are you saying this *namja* without a job is still boyfriend material?"

"*Neh*. More than ever."

Hoon jumped down from the ledge, snatched me up in his strong arms and swung me in a circle.

"*Chung mal?* Tell me. *Chung mal?*"

"Yes. *Chung mal*. Really." I said while my heart shouted that I was mad, crazy, earth-shaking in love with this man!

"*Sah rhang heh*, I love you, my Alice from the moon! How did I ever find you?" With a new urgency, Hoon kissed my brow, my cheek, my lips.

Suddenly, we were bathed in white light. A Watch police cruiser's high-beams held us in its crosshairs. The officer's Brooklyn accent and New York attitude scolded us through her bullhorn. "Hello, young lovers! Yeah, you two, Bruce Lee and Blondie. Take your pillow talk deeper into the First Watch Zone. The good people on my watch are trying to get some sleep!"

Chapter

26: Trading Souls

If a cosmic alchemist took all the energy of Midtown and mixed it with Dexedrine, it still couldn't reach the frenzied atmosphere of Manhattan's Koreatown. The narrow streets were awash with restaurants, coffee shops, *nore-bangs* and clubs. Here, the city of skyscrapers gave way to a town of vertical malls. Each compressed building grew higher and higher to accommodate the burgeoning number of Korean-American consumers.

Hoon seemed to know everyone. As he steered us through the crowd, men and women of all ages came up to nod-bow or shake his hand or both. I had already been educated on conventional Korean greetings.

"Now that you're my *ain*, let me teach you the *Hankook* secret handshake," he said the last time we were in Koreatown. He pointed out two men greeting each other. "See. The younger man will cross his chest with his left arm and tuck his hand near his right under-arm before shaking hands. It's to show respect to your elders."

Hoon's Korean roots were important to him but I noticed that while he followed the rules of *Hankook* etiquette, his affable American smile was offered too.

"There's the place," he stopped in front of a flickering neon bowl of rice. "*Bap muck ja.* Let's eat! A Korean man needs *bap* to recoup."

The pungent odor of fermented cabbage met us in the doorway. My stomach puckered. I felt sick again. While Hoon ordered in Korean, I scanned the noisy eatery for a restroom door. It was beyond a labyrinth of busy tables. I'd wait. I didn't want to be the white girl gagging in the toilet. Maybe a shot of soju would dull the ache.

"Do you know how many drinks are in one bottle of soju?" Hoon asked as he poured two glasses full.

"Too many to remain virtuous?"

"*Kye yup tah*, you're so cute," he said. "There are seven exactly. Want to guess why?"

"I give up," I let him surprise me.

"It's an odd number. Since Koreans always pour each other drinks, they must keep buying. Get it? Two drinkers need at least two bottles."

"Can't two have three drinks each and leave the rest in the bottle?"

"That would be a terrible waste of soju," he feigned sadness.

The volume of the background music was raised to accommodate the growing number of patrons. I recognized the song as the one Hoon programmed into my phone. "That's my ringtone isn't it? What's it called?"

"*Kuh nam jah. That Man.*"

"Pretty melody. Translate the lyrics for me," I asked over the music.

"*Kul seh*, it's about lovers who are so close, they trade souls."

What would Hoon do, when he finds an old wounded soul? I couldn't bear it if he recoiled at the sight me. "I don't think I'd want you to see my soul," I lowered my voice.

"I know." Hoon poured our second round. "You're my Alice from the moon and you have your mysteries."

I was starting to feel the soju's 40-proof when our waiter brought our side dishes.

"This is *oi*, cucumber. Taste it with *bulgogi*, that's the beef." Hoon placed a tidbit of each into my mouth. We had eaten Korean food before and my metal chopstick maneuvers were improving. But it would take me another whole lifetime to figure out how to hold a spoon and chopsticks in one hand as Hoon did.

"*Yogi oh.*" He called for the waiter's attention. "*Go chi jong.*"

A bowl of red pepper paste was brought to our table.

"That's Korean catsup, right?" I recognized the sauce. When we doubled dated with Spencer and Hyun Soo, they dolloped it on every food but dessert.

"*Ah nee. Go chi jong* is our cultural addiction." Hoon deftly made a small package of shredded beef and red pepper paste in a lettuce leaf and fed me.

"I'll make one for you." I put a little mound of beef on lettuce.

"Let's wait a minute." He put down his spoon and chopsticks. "Alice, I've been planning to do this for a while. Maybe I shouldn't until I get another job." He reached for the bottle of soju, changed his mind and took a long gulp from his water glass instead. "Here goes."

Hoon took a small box from his pocket and placed it between us. I stared at the package for so long, he nervously coughed and lifted the lid. Inside was a gold and ruby ring shaped like a bow. I couldn't help myself: I made a girly ooh sound.

Is he giving me a ring? A ring? Yes, oh yes, I'm getting a ring.

"I wanted this ring to say two things to you," he said shyly. "First, it's red because I know you've got this thing about the sky. It's like you're always seeing it for the first time. And second, Alice, you've tied me in knots. If you ever left me, I'd search the world to bring you back."

My real world is so far away. It's crazy to think he'd find me and bring me back.

"Alice!"

I heard my name above the restaurant noise.

"O-M-G, I was just going to text you." Was that Chrissy's voice? I turned around. There she was; same bright smile and huge hoop earrings.

I'd missed her so much but, crap, this was my dream moment. Why did she have to come just then? To make things worse, Chrissy had an entourage of two Asian men and a woman with hair so tightly curled, for a moment I thought she was wearing a hat.

"This is so random." Chrissy's words crashed together in excitement. "My cousin and her boyfriend came down from Connecticut for the week. They just picked me up at JFK last Watch and I was telling them I had to call you. Now we're here and you're here. This is too wakie-crazy."

Hoon's eyes and mine locked. How many words could I fit into a gaze? I'm sorry. They probably won't stay long. He smiled back. It's OK.

"Alice, this is my cousin Samantha and her boyfriend, Ian," Chrissy made her introductions.

Hoon and I rose to introduce ourselves. He signaled a bus boy for more chairs. The screech of the chair legs scraping the floor drowned out the name of the second man.

Chrissy whispered behind her palm, "I see you found yourself a K-boy." She leaned in for a closer look at the ring box on our table. "Nice bling." The six of us squeezed into our seats. Chrissy plucked my ring from its velvet nest and demanded I slip it on. While she and Samantha fussed over my hand, another cramp cinched my belly. I needed to get to the bathroom, but it would be rude to suddenly leave when all eyes were on me.

"Chrissy, would you mind going to the rest room with me?" I whispered. When we stood, Samantha followed our lead. Hoon ordered more soju for the men.

While I waited for the lone stall to be vacant, Chrissy and her cousin took turns trying on my new ring. "Chrissy, this is a special....Why don't I call you next First Watch and tell you everything," I appealed to her sense of romance.

"Don't say another word. I'm completely jealous. He's so gorgeous and he couldn't take his eyes off you," Chrissy turned to her cousin, "You saw it too, didn't you, Samantha."

Samantha's cork-screw curls bobbled when she nodded in agreement. I noticed a family resemblance to Chrissy when her cousin spoke, "I could see it right away. He's wakie-crazy for you.

146

And he looks just like Liu Ye from *The Curse of the Golden Flower*. Doesn't he, Chrissy?" Both cousins gave Hoon two thumbs up.

I loved hearing them praise him. Hoon is a knock-out. He's manly like Bogart in *Casablanca* and charming like Cary Grant in… anything. And I was in a public toilet with women too young to have heard of either of them.

"It's definitely a pre-engagement ring." Chrissy returned the conversation to my ring. "Koreans are big on that. He's saying he's going to propose soon."

He gave me a pre-engagement ring? I pulled out my gloss to daub my lips, but really, I couldn't stop grinning. "Are you sure that's what this means?" I asked.

Chrissy took a heart-shaped compact from her purse to examine her chin. "I'd bet anything."

Like Peg, Chrissy was bright and fun to be with. She was the perfect friend to share Hoon's declaration of love and my ring.

I hadn't expected to fall in love. I certainly couldn't have conceived of being loved and it never occurred to me that Red Sky would come with friends.

"Is your date someone serious?" I asked.

"Curtis? He's cute, right? But, too cheap." Chrissy rummaged through her purse. "Who has Cover-Up?" She probed a spot on her chin. "Not the 'let me buy you a ruby ring' type at all. Definitely not serious."

I gave her my make-up bag. "Someday your prince will come."

"Not till my face clears up! You and Hoon should come to the Asian Alliance Dinner Dance next month. It's a good cause and besides…." She put her finger to her lips. "Shhh, it rocks way past Over Watch."

That might help Hoon job-network. But could I plan for something a month in advance? I hadn't had a scheduled event in Red Sky before. I'd never made a dental appointment or had a pick-up date from a dry cleaner. I didn't even have an address. Was it possible to make plans?

"I'll ask him," I said.

"Ask him now. I'm starving."

A waitress exited the stall and squeezed past us on her way out. I hurried into the vacated stall.

My wad of toilet paper was smeared in red. The next wipe was bloody too. Wasn't staining the first sign of ovarian cancer? I broke into a cold sweat.

"Alice." Chrissy whispered outside the door. "We won't stay long with you guys. We'll let you go celebrate. All by yourselves."

I got her hint but I couldn't have had sex-I was bleeding. A rolling aching cramp jogged my memory of twenty-eight day cycles ending in pain. This is Red Sky and I'm twenty-six. It's just my period. But that means when Hoon and I…I could have gotten…. Oh my God.

"Chrissy, do you have an extra tampon?" I called out.

"No tampons? Don't you dare ruin that fantastic skirt. And please don't say you forgot to take a Blackbird in with you."

"Blackberry?"

Both young women chuckled.

"Alice, you must be the only girl I know who doesn't keep an emergency Blackbird in her bag. I'll get it." I peeked under the hinge to my stall. Chrissy tapped her cell phone on the side of the restroom vending machine. A glossy black package shaped like a bird and no bigger than a deck of cards dropped down. She handed it to me under the door. It contained a pair of black panties with an attached pad, a mini-tampon and vaginal wipes. I cleaned up as best as I could.

Cramps, nausea, periods every month? Just a little while ago, I was complaining about hot flashes.

As I washed my hands, my phone began vibrating and flashing *WATCH* in red. Both Chrissy and her cousin checked their phones. I studied their reactions. They weren't panicking but the signal definitely changed their expressions.

It was probably only a safety check like the ones on TV that say "this is only a test."

We read our texts. The flashing *WATCH* was replaced with a red zipper. "Civil emergency in all First Watch Zones until 2:04 a.m. Please wait for instructions."

"Oh, shit!" Samantha pushed ahead of us towards the door. Chrissy and I followed close behind.

Hadn't we entered the restroom only ten minutes earlier? Why did it feel like a light year ago? The cheerful patter of the patrons, the crisp head nods of the workers, even the clinking of glass on glass morphed into another reality. It was as if in our absence, the Red Sky eatery had become an arena for serious debate. Cell phones beamed their red LED messages at their owners. Wait-staff and diners had joined together in sober discussion groups. It was hideously familiar. I couldn't stifle the images of that early September morning.

I wedged myself between Samantha and Chrissy as we stood outside the restroom. Even flanked by two women who understood the message, I was scared. It must have shown. "Don't be scared, Alice," Chrissy said with conviction. "You're among friends."

My phone, along with everyone else's, sounded three short beeps. I read the new green zipper, "All Clear. For information, check your local news."

I was not reassured.

When the towers fell, I couldn't reach Luke. I dialed and redialed his cell only to hear the same endless silence. I couldn't live that day twice.

Hoon came through the maze of customers and staff to give me a comforting hug. "Come on ladies. I'll escort you back to our table."

Samantha tapped my shoulder. "You've got a prince, Alice."

When we were seated, I held onto my trembling knees.

I could feel Hoon's warm hand top mine as Curtis read his phone aloud.

"Two cops checked out the trunk of a car in front of Penn Station. It was a dud. Just smoke and fizzle. Cops had only minor injuries. Looks like they caught the guys already." He kissed Chrissy's cheek, "who's buying this round?"

Chrissy answered with such an obvious eye-roll that Curtis announced the drinks were on him. We applauded his largess.

Toe-tapping Korean Trot music came back on. Stainless steel chopsticks clicked to the beat as patrons began eating with gusto. A nearby table of women applauded a friend's happy announcement. Curtis placed a twist-off bottle band into my ring box and presented it to Chrissy, making her laugh.

I reached for my water glass. My hands were still shaking.

Hoon noticed. He put down his glass to take my hand. "My *umma* said I had a brave soul. Just for tonight, let's trade souls. I'll give you my brave one and you give me what you can."

I leaned my head on Hoon's shoulder to share his brave soul.

When more *soju* arrived, Curtis filled our glasses. "We should congratulate the new couple."

Hoon and I were beginning another path together. I'd have to reconcile my two lives.

"To Alice and Hoon."

We raised our glasses high above the table.

"*Kom-beh!*"

Chapter

27: The Price of Money

House number 33-33 sat at the end of Manor Road establishing land's end. The four columned red stone colonial had a gable roof and a temple-like entrance. It was likely that this colossal manse had looked out onto Little Neck Bay for a hundred years yet it seemed more suited to the English moors than to be encircled by crushed oyster shell paths and tufts of dune grass. Joseph was sweet to say we were practically neighbors but my part of Queens was blue collar. Douglas Manor housed the rich and famous. Ginger Rogers had once lived on the next street.

I had done the math on Joseph. He'd been traveling for twenty years and began when he was in his fifties. He was at least ten years my senior. Judging from the size of these homes, the Great Pretender could easily afford a personal tanning bed and Barry Manilow's plastic surgeon. All I had was a double coat of under-eye concealer. I didn't want to walk in looking like his grand-mother-come-to-tea. I fluffed up the ruffles on my silk blouse and re-checked my hairdo in the rear-view mirror after turning into the drive.

Why had I called him and accepted his invitation for coffee? Because Joseph De Noto, despite his caveman views of women, was approachable, even likable. Besides, *Mudang* Kim spoke in riddles, making Joseph my sole resource.

I parked on the cobblestone drive that led to a well-tended front garden.

Butterscotch daffodils ran rings around clusters of candy-striped tulips. The scent of homemade grape jam coming from rows of delicate purple hyacinths made it hard to believe I was calling on a steel throttle and parking lot mogul.

Maybe he had a green thumb. More likely a platoon of gardeners. Everywhere I looked was a fresh and dazzling botanical tableau.

The polished mahogany door was opened by a doe-eyed beauty in a starched maid's uniform. "You must be Alice Seaton. Mr. De Noto is expecting you," she said. It was the first time a servant had ever said my name aloud. I thought she would lead me to Joseph but instead she handed me off to a Ms. Ramona who wore a designer celadon silk sheath that I couldn't afford under any color sky.

"I'm Mr. De Noto's personal assistant," she proudly affirmed. Tall and regal, she looked like a runway model. What size was she? Two? Zero?

"He'll be with you in a moment. Why don't you enjoy the afternoon sun in the breakfast room?" she led the way.

Hugh Hefner could surround himself with stunning women in only one world while Joseph kept bevies in two. Remarkable.

I followed her through a pilaster archway into a sunlit room with a view of Little Neck Bay. The room was crowded with black marble tables and weighty wrought iron chairs. I sat in a corner to take it all in. Unlike the subtle garden and organic oyster shell paths, the heavy-handed medieval interior before me reflected Joseph's style.

A white-haired gentleman, his gnarled hands attempting to re-tie the belt of his smoking jacket, entered through the archway. Ms. Ramona was at his elbow, as they slowly made their way to a massive velvet chaise. He must be Joseph's father, I thought. Poor man, he's so frail. I stood to introduce myself. This must be why Joseph didn't sleep in our secret universe. He's been waiting for his dad to pass away before returning for good. If I decided to stay in Red Sky, shouldn't I wait a year or two until Will is settled in Moshi? Is five years long enough? Would there ever be a right time to leave my son?

The elderly gent shook off Ms. Ramona's grip and waved her out of the room. I introduced myself.

"I know who you are, Alice, I guess the old expression in true." He looked me up and down. "A good woman's beauty is eternal. But, as you can see, I'm not up for a little afternoon delight today. Not that I wouldn't try. Too bad you have a boy-friend."

The passing decades may have sanded down his voice but I recognized Joseph's cheeky tone. We sat across from one another at a polished obsidian table. Joseph talked about his three failed marriages. His first wife was a Radio City Music Hall Rockette. The second and third were flight attendants. The maid who met me at the door returned on tiptoe to set down an elaborate Deruta serving plate topped with anisette toast. She poured two cups of aromatic coffee before leaving as quietly as she came. Ms. Ramona followed close behind with two small pills which she left near Joseph's saucer. After finishing his tale about wife number two running off with their dog walker, he took them.

Maybe Joseph wasn't just old. Maybe he was sick. In Red Sky, he had a deep rich tan. Here his skin was as roan and cracked as an English riding saddle.

"So Alice, what can Uncle Joey get you? Fake ID? Passport? School records? Are you really an author? Because if you can string a few words together, I'll get you a publisher," he tempted me.

He could do all that for me? I was several chapters into Blue Skies but could I really be a published novelist?

"Those are all very appealing," I answered. "But before any-thing else happens, I need to know why I travel to Red Sky."

"That's a tough one to answer." Joseph leaned heavily on his elbows to change his position. "I was actively searching for my Red Sky. Maybe, in your heart, you were too."

Is he saying divine intervention let me in because I was searching for Luke?

"Maybe," I answered. If that was true, why hadn't I stopped traveling when I knew he couldn't be found?

"Mostly, I go to escape," he intimated before snapping off a piece of anisette toast and popping it into his mouth. "When I'm there, I feel real." He ran a coil of lemon rind around the rim of his cup.

"I've noticed that too." Had I been looking for the real me all along? Traveling back and forth, changing bodies, how real could I be? I took the rind from my saucer and followed Joseph's lead. The married flavors of coffee and lemon were exquisite. "This is really delicious," I said.

Joseph smoothed the sparse hair at his temples. "You have kids?"

Good grief. Where did that come from? I hadn't considered talking about my sons. After nearly nine years, I still couldn't answer questions about them easily. "I had twins. My son Will is getting married soon. My son Luke was a police officer .... He was killed on 9/11," I finally said.

"I'm sorry for your loss, Alice. Don't mind me, OK? I don't have too many real chin-wags here or in Red Sky." He raised his coffee cup in a salute. "Congratulations to your son Will."

The thought of my Will happily married was heady stuff indeed. "Thank you," I said with a smile.

Joseph finished his anisette toast and washed it down with coffee. "Here's a question I know how to ask. Is there a Mr. Seaton at home?"

"Seaton was my maiden name." I wasn't bringing any more about Mike into this conversation. Even if Joseph knew things about me that no one else knew, I wasn't comfortable sharing my thoughts about leaving my husband. "Joseph, what you said when we first met, is it true? I just have to spend the night in Red Sky to stay there?"

"Yep. I call it the fairy tale feature. See, the seeds keep you young while you're in Red Sky, providing you don't sleep there. And when

I say sleep, I mean all night. You can nod off for a few minutes, but no longer than that." He waggled a gnarled finger in front of my face. "Don't forget. Once you sleep there, your internal clock re-sets. You're just another Red Sky girl and you'll grow old all over again."

That was fine with me. I didn't want to stay young while Hoon grew older. I'd look forward to each stage of life if we could share them.

"Growing old is not necessarily a bad thing, Joseph. Why haven't you stayed?"

He studied the backs of his hands. His knuckles looked metallic as if the bones beneath his skin were made of bronze. I finished my coffee to keep from staring.

"Ever hear of Addison's disease?" he asked.

"No."

"Lucky you. It's a hormonal disorder. I've had it almost fifty years. You become an expert on a disease once you have it," he rubbed the back of one hand with his other.

I reflected on my own experience. Will's diagnosis had made me an authority on Asperger's. Eventually, I learned Will's strengths but Mike couldn't get past his weaknesses. Not that I handled our challenges well, too often I had depended on Luke for moral support. The memories of using one son to lighten the burdens of the other still weighed heavy on me.

Joseph's hand shook as he poured us each another half cup of coffee. "Addison's isn't terminal, but it made me its prisoner. When I have an attack, the docs call it a crisis, I have to be hospitalized."

"I'm sorry this happened to you, Joseph. It's exhausting fighting an illness year after year," I knew too well.

"Damn right, it is. Traveling can't erase a disease if you get it before you turn twenty-six. I was diagnosed in college. Shitty, huh?" he shrugged.

At twenty-six, I was pregnant with my boys. Other than swollen ankles and a craving for Fudgesicles, I was in perfect health. My parents were right: Healthy is better than wealthy.

"There's no cure in either universe." Joseph reached for the last anisette toast. "That's why I don't sleep in Red Sky. I don't need another forty or fifty years of attacks. It's better that I stay a traveler. That way, if I start to feel sick, I can go home. Besides," he pointed to his knuckles, "I'm tired of seeing my skin the color of rust."

I covered his hands with mine.

"You're a sweet lady, Alice," his voice softened. "You've got… what's that Yiddish word? I dated a Jewish girl back in the sixties… *rach-mon-is!* Real empathy for others."

His cell phone played *Nessam Dorma*. Joseph ignored it. "They'll call back." He leaned closer to me. "From the first time I went to Red Sky to the night I met you, I'd been hoping to meet another traveler. You can't imagine what I pictured—super models, movie stars, whole towns of travelers. I'm glad it was you."

"I'm glad too."

"Let's stay friends. You can pick the universe. I'm OK with your choice," he smiled like young Joseph.

I placed my napkin on my plate and stood. "Thank you so much for this afternoon."

"Wait a sec." He put up his hand. "Actually, I invited you here because something you said doesn't sit right with me. How do you have a friend who gives such an expensive gift?"

Through the high vaulted windows, dark and heavy clouds mauled the sun. Their shadows, like secrets, twisted the light. Laura was still working part time to make ends meet. She couldn't have splurged on my birthday gift.

"Why? Are the seeds that costly?" I asked.

"Costly? Let me put it this way, either your friend hit Powerball or her hubby dropped dead and left her a fortune. We're talking about a million dollars a visit," Joseph rose from his chair.

A million? Impossible. "You visited a *mudang* twenty years ago, Joseph. Maybe now seeds are cheaper. Cheap."

He tossed his napkin on to the table. "Twenty years ago, twenty minutes ago, that never happens."

I slipped my arm through my purse straps. "Are you sure?"

"No one gets those seeds without a million, Alice. No one."

무궁화

I sat behind the wheel with my keys still in hand asking myself where Laura would get a million dollars. Whatever savings she might have had were cleaned out by her ex-husband. I remembered too well the afternoon she sat bawling her eyes out at my kitchen table. After he had closed all their accounts, she worked two jobs to make up the loss. Collecting Social Security hadn't made her rich. That was for darn sure.

I started my car and re-adjusted the rearview mirror. Laura's a super shopper. Maybe she out-haggled Mr. Kim. I massaged my temples to help me think. I couldn't picture her besting the old *mudang*. Then again, I couldn't picture her sleeping with my husband.

The tire treads crunched and crackled over Joseph's driveway.

Had Laura convinced Mike to pay for the seeds? With what? His pension?

My grip tightened on the gear shift as it finally hit me. Mike and I had been given a fortune—Luke's 9/11 Compensation Fund. The money we had put aside for Will's future- *2.2 million dollars.*

28: Pure as Gold

Hell week was finally over. It had begun with a pencil-necked bank manager painstakingly explaining that any of the parties named on Will's trust account could make changes. As proof, he placed copies of online transfers in front of me and tapped his pen point on each one. For two years, Mike had made withdrawals in increments of $9,616.00 until a month before my last birthday. His total withdrawals added up to a million dollars. The same Mike who couldn't find the backspace key on a laptop had figured out how to cyber-steal from his own son.

Before the week ended, I had met with three more bank managers and my accountant. On Friday, after Will and I picked up his wedding suit from the tailor's, we spent the rest of the morning signing papers to protect his funds. Mike would find out soon enough but he wouldn't be able to do a damn thing about it.

"Why did we have to change banks?" Will asked as we drove out of the parking lot.

Was Will suspicious? Or just anxious the way Asperger sufferers get from sudden changes?

"A married man should handle his own accounts," I answered. "Don't worry. We've put everything in place now. When you get to Moshi, if you have any questions or problems you can contact your accountant through email. You can even Skype her."

159

"Mom, I'm an *Aspy*, not mentally retarded. I get all that. I'm asking why we didn't we stay at the same bank. Does the Bank of Queens give more interest than Floral Park Family Bank? It's important to get the most interest and the best loan rates. The highest online bank offers 1.2%," he said.

Thank goodness. Will was merely processing his facts. He hadn't suspected his dad had pocketed his funds. And why would he? Look how long it took me to figure it out. "Yes, they give the best interest and your money is totally safe," I assured him.

We were nearing the Lake Success Mall. At the traffic signal, I watched as a line of cars turned into the west entrance. Lunchtime traffic was picking up. "Should we stop for pizza before getting your wedding bands?" I asked.

"Can't. Sorry. I have to be back at the veterinary clinic at one. I'm cleaning Rosco the dachshund's teeth. Dachshunds have more periodontal disease than other breeds."

Lunch with me had come in second to a dog's gum problems. Peg was right after all—eventually, mothering was done. It was a liberating revelation.

The security system at *Silver's Gold Mine Jewelers* buzzed us in. Mr. Silver, gnome-shaped with untamed eyebrows and a beak nose raised his head from his work. He lifted one bushy brow to release the jeweler's loupe from his eye and caught it in his palm. Had he not been dressed in suit and tie, he could have passed for Snow White's Grumpy. Why had Will picked this shop?

The jeweler's broad smile instantly softened his features. "Look who's here, handsome Mr. Pleasance and his first love," he shook Will's hand and offered me coffee.

I was stressed and tired after all our errands. The last thing I needed was caffeine. "No thanks. We're just here to pick up my son's bands," I answered curtly.

At least, have a seat," the jeweler fetched a chair for me.

I took it gratefully.

"Your son, what a boy. Nice, polite, not to mention a regular encyclopedia on animals." He reached behind the counter to buzz in another customer. "Phillip!" he shouted to the back of the store. "Mr. Mogeloff is here for a pick-up."

A young worker with remnants of lunch at the corners of his mouth rushed in with a gold watchband dangling from his hand.

Mr. Silver kept a vigilant eye on his helper until he was sure that Mr. Mogeloff was a satisfied customer. Then he opened a velveteen box and handed it to Will. "So, Mr. Pleasance, what do you think?"

"Do they have our initials?" Will's smile widened.

"Look for yourself. Better your opinion than a stranger's." Mr. Silver removed the rings from the box.

Will held them like coins. "Look Mom, my initials are in Ruthie's ring and hers are in mine." His joy nearly brought me to tears. I stepped up to the counter. The simple white metal bands sparkled under the store's bright lights.

"What a lovely idea," I told my son, but it was more than lovely–it was utterly romantic.

"Ruthie thought of it." He examined each ring. "Ruthie's dad asked us to buy plain ones. The people in Moshi are very poor. We have to respect their feelings." Will slipped on his ring. "I wanted plain anyway."

I understood Mr. Cole's reasoning but was the jeweler honest? Had he seen Will as someone who'd think an inexpensive silver band was white gold?

"Are these silver?" I questioned.

The jeweler's eyebrows knitted together at my insult. "Take a look inside. See 14K. Who gets married in silver? Navahos?"

My long day had taken its toll. I had just been rude to someone who was courteous and respectful to my son. "I'm so sorry. I was concerned," I quickly apologized.

"Don't worry yourself," he comforted me. "I've been in business since 1969. Mothers of the brides are even worse. They all want big diamonds no matter what kind of son-in-law they're getting. But Mr. Pleasance, here…"

Will returned the rings to the box and looked directly at the jeweler. Mr. Silver patted Will's shoulder. "He's the diamond!"

Will laughed. Except for family and Ruthie, I hadn't seen him look anyone in the eyes before. I'd never even witnessed Will understand a joke. Truthfully, I had always been so worried about him I doubted I really saw him at all.

I stroked Will's cheek. "You *are* a diamond."

"That's an interesting ring you have, Missus. May I take a look?" the jeweler extended his hand.

I turned my ring from Hoon several times till it loosened. It was tighter on me in daytime. I had only taken it off once before, to look at it under a bright blue sky. My ruby ring was the tangible link between Hoon's world and my world, between Hoon and me.

Mr. Silver examined it under his loupe. He wiped it with a cloth and studied it again. Then he weighed it. When he read his little scale, he shook his head. "This, I never saw before. Would you mind if I tested it?" he asked. It was only a formality; in a second, he was rubbing the edge of my ring on a whetstone until it left a narrow golden stripe. "I won't damage it," he promised before taking a small plastic bottle marked Nitric Acid and applying a drop to the stripe. "See, no change. This is 18 karat gold."

"Are the rubies real?" I had to ask.

"The rubies are triple A. Beautiful. I thought maybe it's an antique but the cut and setting are modern. And the maker's mark inside," Mr. Silver rubbed his hand over the back of his neck, "I never saw markings like these. It's not American. Definitely not European. This ring, it's like it's from another planet."

The store phone rang like an alarm.

Phillip asked the caller to hold. "Mr. Silver, Mrs. Sweeny wants to know if her bracelet is ready."

"Her bracelet is sitting here for a week already. Tell her to come now. And Phillip, ring up Mr. Pleasance's wedding bands. Don't forget to put the warranty card inside." He looked my way and winked.

Will left for the cash register.

The jeweler put his loupe down on the counter and handed back my ring. "Rubies come from the Far East. Sometimes gold is smuggled through Asia. Maybe your ring's from Red China," he said.

Not Red China, Mr. Silver. Red Sky. I put my purse on the counter top and asked, "Would you show me men's rings? I'm looking for a simple white gold band with a small blue stone. Sky blue."

Chapter

29: The Best Laid Schemes

I had only a half hour to get to Tribeca Rooftop for Hoon's installation as the managing director of the Korean American Charities Council. Since the car bomb attack last month, there had been several temporary Watch Zone changes. The re-routing made getting around Manhattan a test of patience as police cones blocked many familiar avenues. Why had I let Chrissy convince me to get ready at her mom's shop?

"Alice, Koreans really dress-up for these events," she couldn't contain her excitement. "I have tons of drop-dead clothes from Hong Kong. Come here first. I know a great place to get your nails done too."

In Chinatown, Chrissy and her friends poured me into a black sequined dress, twirled my wild hair into a French braid and crammed my pedicured feet into rhinestone studded heels. She wouldn't let me get into my cab until they had posted my metamorphosis on her Facebook page. Happily what happened in Red Sky stayed in Red Sky.

무궁화

When the double elevator doors opened, I knew that Chrissy was right. The atrium was filled with dapper patrons in tuxedos and beautiful women in dazzling gowns. Hoon was circled by well-wishers. He moved like an aristocrat in his dinner jacket as he shook hands and bowed to his elders.

I managed to catch Hoon's eye. He mimed a kiss. As he wound his way to the elevator bank, a bespectacled gentleman took his arm and introduced him to another group waiting to congratulate him. He beckoned over his shoulder as they led him away.

When Hoon was hired, we celebrated with champagne. "I'll earn less than half of what I made at LB, Alice. We won't have too many bottles of top shelf in our future," he apologized.

"I won't miss it."

"After college, all I wanted to make was money. Now, I want to make things right. Does that sound crazy?" he asked.

"Not as long as you keep trying to make things right." I had found a great guy who's also a good man. So what if it took me two lifetimes.

The hem of my dress pressed against my thighs as I made my way across the room. I breathed in my own perfume. My heart beat quickened as I watched Hoon. This must be what it means to live in the moment. Before Hoon, I had allowed myself to take a long dark tea time of the soul rather than live. It was a mistake I wouldn't make again. I didn't want to be without this man. God forgive me, I didn't.

I had planned to give Hoon the ring after his installation. I squeezed my borrowed silk clutch to feel the gift box tucked inside. In a little while, my ring would be on his finger.

"Are you Miss Alice?" A soft voice and the whisper of flowing silk broke into my thoughts. I turned towards a diminutive, pinch-faced woman in a delicate pink hanbok. The traditional Korean dress billowed around her like a Red Sky cloud.

"Yes."

"Please speak in full sentences. I want to hear your enunciation," she demanded.

Why? "Yes. I'm Alice and you are?"

"I'm Dr. Buja Hong, the director of education at KACC." She handed me her business card.

Should I get business cards too? Something snappy. *Alice Seaton. Part time writer. Full time universe traveler.* Dr. Hong didn't look like the type who'd enjoy my joke.

"You're a college graduate. English literature, yes?" she asked while scrutinizing my outfit.

"Yes, Dr. Hong. I am." How did she know?

"Nicely put. Managing Director Park said you are well mannered. So many Caucasians are not," she sniffed.

Well, feel free to say any little racist remark that pops into your head, I thought.

"We at Korean-American Charities Council have a high enrollment of older women returning to the work force who need to learn English from a native speaker. I'm looking for someone to fill the position. Would you be interested in applying?" she asked.

"Yes." Full sentences, remember. "Yes, I would be quite interested."

Dr. Hong took a prickling peek at my short hemline. "KACC has a reputation to maintain so no gum chewing or casual clothing. It is most important that the person we hire respects her elders," she made her point.

A career in Red Sky? Somebody pinch me. Could I really get paid to steep myself in English with women at an age I knew like the back of my hand, literally? As enticing as it sounded, I suspected in a short while the very direct Dr. Hong was going to ask me career related questions like the ones I pictured in my mind:

How much experience do you have?

At teaching or at being old?

When did you graduate?

Probably the same year you did. Go, class of '69!

I doubt that I'd get the job.

Together, Dr. Hong and I headed for the crowded lounge. Networking guests had already clogged the passageway, balancing one-bite canapés and jumbo wine glasses in their hands. A gala in Manhattan was really LinkedIn in party clothes. Dr. Hong beckoned to the man I'd seen with Hoon earlier. "There's my husband. He's bringing Managing Director Park," she nodded in their direction.

Hoon greeted Dr. Hong in Korean as he bowed low. I knew that meant she was not only an elder but also a power player at Korean-American Charities Council.

"He's so busy tonight," Dr. Hong said as she patted Hoon's arm.

Had Hoon known about her job offer? Probably. "Yes, Managing Director Park has been very busy." I turned to Hoon and grinned. "Hasn't he?"

"*O mon ah!*" Dr. Hong's husband looked at me strangely. "*Yo bo,*" he addressed his wife. "Don't you see it?" He didn't wait for her answer. "Look at her face," he urged. They began speaking in rapid fire Korean. Did they know me? Were they travelers too? I was being paranoid. Joseph said I was the only traveler he'd met in twenty years.

"Managing Director Park, didn't you notice the resemblance to *Palan Nun Ahgesshi?*" Dr. Hong's husband asked Hoon.

"I've only seen her portrait in *Bang mul gwan* once when I visited Korea as a child, sir." Hoon took in my features. "But you may be right about the resemblance."

The couple lapsed into Korean again. I didn't like being the foreigner. Red Sky or not, this was still America.

Hoon touched my arm. "Alice, this is Dr. Joon Kang, Dr. Hong's husband. He's saying you resemble the portrait of the Blue-eyed Mission Girl from an old Joseon folk tale."

I dipped my head down and extended my hand to cover all ethnic etiquette bases.

"The Blue-eyed Mission Girl is part of our history," Dr. Hong reproached Hoon, "not a folktale."

"You look exactly like *Palan Nun Aghesshi*," Dr. Kang said after shaking my hand. "It's extraordinary." He turned to Hoon. "Let's find seats."

A corner cocktail table became available. Hoon quickly moved chairs out for the doctors and me. Dr. Kang looked for something on his cell phone. "*Bo seh yo.* Take a look."

His screen showed a young woman with a braided black wig atop her blonde hair. Where had I seen that portrait before? Her hairpiece was festooned with bejeweled combs and her *hanbok* was embroidered in shimmering threads.

Like me, she was fair and blue-eyed but I didn't think the resemblance was uncanny.

Hoon translated the web page aloud. "During the late Joseon Era, an English missionary was asked to tutor King Cheoljong's sickly son. The missionary brought his wife and daughter with him to live on the King's land. The peasants loved the young girl for her giving nature and called her *Palan Nun Aghesshi*, Blue-eyed Girl. Soon, the prince fell in love with her."

"Blue eyes are common among Northern Europeans," I said as I inched my chair closer to Hoon's. "But tell me, Hoon, do all European-Americans look alike to you?" He pressed his knee into mine. I understood and stopped teasing.

"Go on, *Hoon Yi Sa*. Your Alice should learn our history." Dr. Hong patted my hand affectionately.

"When the Queen found out that her son loved a Westerner, she ordered the girl's beheading. The frantic prince decreed that any *mudang* who could call the spirits to save *Palan Nun Aghesshi* would be rewarded beyond her wildest dreams." Hoon continued.

Her wildest dreams? Is *Mudang* Kim an imposter? "Aren't all *mudangs* men?" I asked.

Dr. Kang slapped his hand on the table. "What a remarkable girl you are! Not many white people have even heard of *mudangs*," he elbowed his wife.

Dr. Hong's stern demeanor softened. "Very impressive, young lady. In its beginnings, Korean shamanism used *mudangs* to act as intermediaries between the gods and humans. Back then all *mudangs* were women.

"And now?" I asked, wondering what to make of this new information.

"Now?" Dr. Hong shrugged. "Sadly, now, like so much of the world, anybody can be anything, talented or not. I've heard shaman lineage has been so corrupted that modern *mudangs* aren't very skillful and some are quite mad," she confided her last words in a whisper.

That would explain why *Mudang* Kim files his nails to look like eagle claws and talks in riddles. I thought

"Please go on, Hoon Yi Sa," Dr. Hoon directed.

"A thousand troops rode though the countryside until they returned with Joseon's most revered *mudang*, Hoon continued. "Under a harvest moon, she fed the girl seeds that made her age forty years overnight. The next morning, when the palace guards opened the lock on *Palan Nun Aghesshi's* bamboo cell, the girl was gone. In her place was an old missionary woman fast asleep."

That was too close to my reality. Could *Palan Nun Aghesshi* be my relative? Was this the Korean ancestor Joseph mentioned when we met in his parking lot? "Does the article reveal her Christian name?" I asked Hoon.

Hoon scrolled down. "I don't think so."

Had the Blue-eyed Girl been a Seaton? Or a Carne on my mother's side? Was I her descendant? I already knew the answer: I had no blood relations in Red Sky.

Dr. Kang tried to flag a waitress with a tray of champagne flutes then signaled Hoon to read on.

"According to the historic journals of the *Andong Kim* clan, rumors spread that the royal *gama* carrying the prince stopped on the pier where a ship was about to board a missionary couple and an old woman." Dr. Hong signaled Hoon to stop. "Alice, my dear, in ancient times, royalty travelled in wooden seating rooms called *gamas* that were carried by slaves," she turned to Hoon. "*Hoon Yi Sa,* you must teach Alice to speak Korean."

Hoon nodded in agreement and continued. "A royal guard escorted the old woman to the *gama* and then ordered everyone on the pier to turn and face the sea. After a few moments, the old woman returned to board the ship and the *gama* with its royal entourage was gone. Later, the Queen's soldiers arrived to question witnesses. One by one, they claimed they had only looked out on the sea and one by one they were executed. Years passed, but still the disappearance of *Palan Nun Aghesshi* was talked about in whispers. One winter, a plague felled most of the king's slaves. An old gama carrier, sickened and dying, confessed he witnessed the last conversation between the prince and *Palan Nun Aghesshi*. He swore the prince wept when the old woman said, 'do not cry, my beloved, but remember this: I will not miss my youth as much as I will miss you.'" Hoon finished his reading.

Dr. Kang pointed his finger at me. "There's no love like Korean love and looking at you Alice, makes me think *Palan Nun Aghesshi* has returned to reclaim her prince."

Do they really believe I'm the Blue-eyed Girl incarnate? Did Hoon believe it too?

"Why didn't the prince try to get her back?" I asked.

Dr. Hong answered, "He was the heir to the throne, dear. He could hardly go off with an old white-skinned commoner, but then again, *sarang eui gijeok*," she dismissed my question.

What was that supposed to mean? The three of them shared her joke and left me out. Was I laughable for questioning a scene from their dopey fairy-tale? Where the heck was the cocktail waitress? Why can't you find one when you need a drink. Still, if all this was true, even a little true, I wished the prince loved his blue-eyed girl even after she had aged forty years.

Hoon returned Dr. Kang's phone and reached for my hand. We intertwined our fingers.

"Hoon, in the story, when she turned old," I lowered my voice, "did the prince love her just as passionately?"

"It's only a folktale, Alice." He eyed Dr. Kang's empty glass. "Ready for another, sir?"

I freed my hand from Hoon's. The fate of *Palan Nun Aghesshi*, doomed to spend her youth as an old woman gnawed at my heart. I guessed Koreans didn't need their stories to have happy endings. But I did.

It may have been childish, but the desire to see my ring on Hoon's hand had waned. He wouldn't get his gift tonight. The plans of mice and men and blue-eyed girls often go awry.

Chapter

30: A New Way of Looking at the World

Morning sunlight poured through the kitchen blinds and onto the table while I worked at my new netbook. I had transferred *Blue Skies* to WordPad in order to begin a stricter writing routine. The first draft of chapter twelve was finished. I checked the time at the bottom of the screen. In a little while, Mike would come down the stairs with a clean shirt and a dirty rotten lie. Most days his excuse to slink off to Laura's was a visit to Auntie's but occasionally it was off-the-cuff hogwash. I snapped the blinds shut. Had this whole ruse been concocted to get Will's money?

"Alice, is my seersucker jacket back from the cleaners?" he shouted from the top of the stairs.

"Inside the closet door," I called back out of habit. "Are you going out?"

"Didn't I tell you? I'm meeting up with a couple of guys I used to know at work," he lied.

I closed the netbook. Upstairs, Mike whistled a Beatles song. He had found his jacket. Why was he dawdling?

I went into the bathroom, locked the door and waited for the sound of the front door closing. When would I split from Mike and tell Hoon the truth? The night at the Tribeca Rooftop had put everything on hold. Hoon's attitude toward the story about the young prince was a wake-up call: No young man would want an old woman's love.

This wasn't the time for decisions. I grabbed the loofa and turned on the shower. Right now, I was the mother-of-the-groom with an appointment for a fitting. After exfoliating my skin till it burned, I shut off the water, wrapped a towel around me and dripped dry on the mat. Nothing had been resolved but at least I was clean.

무궁화

Big and bubbly Arva, the owner of Paris Designs, was from the Dominican Republic and had probably never been to France. But she charmed every customer from bat-mitzvah girls to grandmas-of-the-brides. The shop walls were chock-a-block full of glittering gowns that rained loose sequins on the floor until it looked like a star-filled night. Arva took a pin from her mouth, stuck it into her pin cushion wristlet, and greeted me with a hug.

"Mommy, I just pressed your dress," she said. "So gorgeous. Come to the back. We'll try it on one more time."

I hadn't wanted to go to my final fitting alone, but Peg was visiting her sister in Boston and Ilene was babysitting Caulder. I would have asked Laura but she was probably still in bed…with Mike.

I stepped up on the box in front of a high three paneled mirror. If nothing else, the stress of a cheating husband had got me down another few pounds to reveal a small waist I thought had disappeared forever. My celadon sheath, even though it was made of rayon in China, made me look nearly as sophisticated as Joseph's Ms. Ramona.

"See, it fits beautiful now. Let me get the wrap." Arva left me with my three images. We all had crow's feet. This is who I really am. Hoon couldn't love this. I burst into tears.

Each time I tried to choke down a sob, I began again. Arva slipped a wrinkled Kleenex to me through the curtains. "Let it out, mommy," she said. "Most women cry before a wedding and they all cry after they're married. Right?" I chuckled in spite of my misery.

"Look, I got nobody coming in until my one o'clock today," she said as she slid the curtain back. "You want to talk, we talk. You want to cry? We gotta get you changed first." Arva undid the buttons at the back of my neck. "You get tears on this, we got more problems." She pulled the dress over my head avoiding the mascara tracks on my cheeks. "You take all the time you need," she said before leaving me alone with my images.

At the cash register, I unloaded my last ten years on Arva's ample shoulders. I told her how I had lost my child on 9/11, that my husband and my friend were having an affair and that right now they were probably in the bed I had helped her pick out at Sleepy's. Then I finally wound down like a clock-work toy.

"Dios mio, Dios mio," Arva said as she handed me a paper cup of water. "Mommy, you gotta throw him out. I don't know what's wrong with American women. They stay in these dead marriages until it kills them. You're a good looking woman. Go get yourself a nice man."

"I already have a nice man." Now why did I say that? I downed my water.

"So what are you gonna do?" Arva asked as she tenderly folded my dress and wrap into a Paris Design box.

Staying with Mike was no longer an option. I deserved better. I knew that. And as for my darling Will, his future as a missionary in Moshi with a loving wife and family was the answer to my prayers. But what about Hoon?

I put the empty cup on the counter. Was I really free to decide things for myself? "I'll figure it out," I said as we hugged goodbye. "Thank you, Arva, for *everything*." I tucked my dress box under my arm and headed outside to face my future.

무궁화

I spent four days putting the rest of my wedding ensemble together, most of that time spent in search of toeless pantyhose.

On Saturday, when I knew Mike was at Laura's, I lugged a suitcase down from the attic. Inside, I packed seven of his T-shirts, seven briefs, his flip-flops and dress shoes. I stuffed seven pairs of socks in the side bag then neatly folded in his chinos, and a good suit along with two dress shirts and ties. I collected his toiletries from the bathroom, put them in a plastic bag, and zipped the suitcase shut. It wasn't easy to drag it downstairs but eventually, one small step at a time, I got it to the side door. How appropriate, I thought. This is where I usually set the bags of garbage before opening the door and throwing them out.

When Mike returned, he didn't notice the suitcase. "I'm going upstairs to take a nap," he muttered. I smelled Laura's shampoo on him. At least he had the decency to wash her off before entering my house.

I stood riveted in the doorway while my mind raced. Why had it taken me nine full months to sort it all out? Seeds for a birthday gift. Dreams that weren't dreams. And that afternoon when Joseph asked me what kind of woman gives away eternal youth—the answer should have hit me—the kind of woman who lived next door, offered to carpool, and slept with my husband.

In the kitchen, I made an iced black coffee. It could have used a shot of soju. Instead, I added more ice and gulped it down before walking across Laura's lawn.

"Hey, you home?" I called through the screen door before letting myself in.

Laura was in her robe, fresh from her own shower. There it was; that same whiff of Herbal Essence. "Showering at this time of the day? Were you cleaning up after a little afternoon delight?" I sniggered.

"What?" Her cheeks flushed. Finally, an indication that she was capable of shame.

"Come for tea," I said as sweetly as I could muster.

"I'm still in my bathrobe." Laura tied her belt tighter and kept her hands on its ends. Was it my imagination or was she actually uneasy in my presence?

"I'll wait while you get dressed. Besides, I picked up a little something for you," I posed a smile.

"Give me five minutes to change," she headed for her bedroom. Laura never could turn down a freebie.

무궁화

Mike was still napping upstairs when I ushered Laura into my kitchen. "Take a seat at the table. Tea will be ready in a minute." I put the kettle on and opened a cabinet door. "I know there's a box of Lipton's in here somewhere." I called over my shoulder.

Laura sat with her hands folded. Bold as brass, my mother would have said. I brought our mugs of tea to the table with a gift-wrapped package.

"What's this?" Laura asked.

"Just a little present. I wanted to thank you for my Korean seeds," I kept up my pretense.

"How sweet." She pulled on the taped ends of the wrapping. "The seeds were for your birthday. You really shouldn't have."

Laura tore away the paper to reveal a copy of the 3D puzzle book; *Magic Eye: A New Way of Looking at the World.* "Oh cute," she said. "I haven't seen one of these in a while."

Without opening it, she placed the book on the empty seat beside her.

"Come on, Laura, you've *never* seen a magic eye picture," I baited her.

"That's silly. We had the books at home. Our kids played with them all the time," she kept up her own pretenses.

"So the inscrutable *Mudang* Kim didn't tell you that entering a parallel universe is just like adjusting your eyes to see the hidden pictures in those puzzles," I grew angrier by the second. "That means people like you, people with strabismus, can't see it while people like me can."

Laura stirred her tea. The tinny chiming of her spoon on porcelain grew faster.

I wasn't finished. "You told me that you had tried the seeds. Did you and Mike plan to meet in your own private universe? How disappointing!" I hadn't known it before but as soon as I said the words, I knew the truth. Everything Mike had done—stealing Will's money, lying to me—was for Laura. Then when they realized Laura couldn't leave this world, he chose to stay with her. I needed to vomit but I gulped hard and waited for her admission.

Laura let go of her teaspoon and fingered her shower-damp hair but no amount of delaying erased the look of guilt from her face.

"It's not really what you think," she said without looking up.

"Yes it is. It's exactly what I think."

Maybe I should have forgiven them their trespasses. After all, I had been cheating on Mike from the moment I met Hoon. But they had stolen from my son, and I wanted some Old Testament retribution. I walked to the bottom of the stairs and yelled like the house was on fire. "Mike! Come down here, quick! There's a rat in the kitchen!"

By the time he stomped down the steps, I had taken the box of Lipton's from the counter and thrown it in the trash.

Chapter

31: My Best Friend on Earth

Swing the Teapot Restaurant in Floral Park was my choice for Peg's birthday luncheon. The tables and chairs came from tag sales and salvage yards, the waitstaff was fresh from County Mayo, and the food was hearty. I sent out vintage invitations and entitled the party, "Old Is the new New!" I had scored four little 1950s plastic birthday baskets from eBay and filled them with penny candies although I wasn't sure Laura would join us.

Mike had moved into Auntie's after I handed him his suitcase. I was probably as surprised as he was that Laura didn't invite him to live with her. I guess she only wanted a man sharing her life, not her bathroom.

The day after I confronted them, I called Ilene and told her about Mike and Laura. She was driving Nick to his chemotherapy appointment but tried her best to be supportive and comforting. Then I called Peg. "Mike and Laura are having an affair." I announced.

"Holy heck, Alice," she shouted into the phone. "Are you sure?"

"I confronted them yesterday," I assured her.

"Holy shit."

By the time I told Peg about Mike stealing Will's money so they could run-off, she had run out of *holies*. Still, I didn't tell her everything. I didn't mention the seeds.

"Jesus forgive me, but I should have seen it," Peg confessed. "I never liked her, not since the first day at Tiny Tots Nursery School when she showed up in a mini-skirt, reeking of drug store perfume and desperation. Don't you dare speak to her again. As soon as we hang up, I'm disinviting that tramp from my party."

"Don't. It'll be more fun to see her uncomfortable," I was almost gleeful. "Besides, I want Ilene, you and me to be civilized."

"You're not letting her come to Will's wedding, Alice?"

"I said *civilized* Peg, not saintly. Laura could piss up a rope before I'd let that happen," I meant every word I had just said.

By the time Laura arrived at the party, Ilene, Peg and I were working on our first pints of Guinness Stout. Laura acted like nothing had changed, and we three kept up the charade.

We gorged ourselves on smoked salmon sandwiches and washed them down with more ale on tap. "I haven't seen a spread like this since my Ma's wake. You did a fine job for an English girl," Peg said after wiping foam from the tip of her nose.

Ilene asked the waitress to take our picture and mugged for the camera with wax lips candy in her mouth.

"Let me take a picture of you, Ilene." I said.

"Just me?"

"There's no *just* about you," I protested. "You're a good friend and the world's greatest grandma. Besides, most women can't pull it off but you look beautiful in wax lips."

"I know. I'm styl'n." Ilene grinned for my photo.

"You go, girl!" I saved her picture in my phone.

After our luncheon plates were cleared, Peg modeled the watch her husband had bought for her birthday. We complimented his good taste in watches and wives. Ilene asked if anyone had tried the new frozen yogurt shop in the Lake Success Mall. Laura said she had. Peg and I said we hadn't. It was a conversation of short sentences punctuated by what wasn't said.

Our waitress returned with a three tiered tray of pastries. She poured Irish tea for us from a steaming Parian Ware pot and asked if we needed anything else. Her bright blue eyes and soft blonde hair reminded me of *Palan Nun Aghesshi*. If only I could have brought Dr. Hong and her husband here to prove that Westerners had no shortage of girls who looked like younger versions of me.

The day before, I had spent hours online slogging through Korean history. King Cheoljong and Queen Cheolin's sons had died in infancy, and while there may have been hundreds of blue-eyed daughters of missionaries, none of them were famous. There wasn't even a hint of *Palan Nun Aghesshi* in my day world.

But later that night, on my bus ride to meet Hoon, I googled her name on my phone. Her portrait popped up on a dozen sites. She really was a legend in Red Sky. Versions of the Blue-eyed Girl story contained lots of passion but skimped on historical details. "The prince cried out his undying love for the bewitched old woman on the pier," one article said, but no seaport was named. Even the year of the event was absent from the accounts.

Our party was coming to a close. I added a trickle of cream to my tea and stirred until it turned a warm caramel. If there was an actual *Palan Nun Aghesshi* in Red Sky, her biography, like her black wig, was richly embellished.

Ilene called out "It's birthday present time!" as she rifled through her big crocheted tote. Eventually she found the Book Nook gift card for Peg. "I knew it was in here somewhere."

"This is perfect, Ilene. As soon as classes are over, I'm getting a trashy summer read," Peg said and kissed the air between them.

Laura passed a flowery wrapped box to Peg.

"The gift wrap is beautiful," Ilene said as she pulled down her reading glasses from the top of her head for a closer look. "Where did you find it?"

"It's from France," Laura bragged.

But I knew it was from a yard sale.

"Open it at home, Peg," Laura said airily. "Then you can save the gift wrap."

Peg tore off the paper to annoy Laura, and removed a Mondrian-inspired silk scarf. "Thank you. It's very pretty," she said.

I thought so too, especially since I had bought it for Laura two Christmases ago. No wonder she didn't want Peg to open it at the table. Laura didn't seem to know any of the conventions of polite society—no re-gifting in front of the first purchaser, no nickel-and-diming hard working waitstaff, and most important of all, hands off your friend's husband's tool-set. I drank my tea to calm down, reminding myself to let it go. This party was about making Peg happy.

I handed Peg her gift. "You are the best friend a woman could have," I said as I watched Laura squirm in her chair. Her discomfort inspired me to heap more praise on Peg. "You're smart, sincere, and always ready to offer a shoulder or lend an ear. I am blessed to know you. May you have good health and happiness for the rest of your days."

Peg un-wrapped the Coach waist purse and a small bottle of Tasmanian Rain Water. "Wait until my daughters see these," she said as she opened the water bottle. Then she daubed a drop on the back of her wrist and breathed it in. "Ah, smells like what rich people drink." She kissed my cheek and whispered, "Thanks for my fashionable purse, decadently expensive water and the best birthday party ever."

I tapped the side of my water glass with a fork for their attention. "I have something for all of us. To the *former* Carlucci's Birthday Dinner Club members," I said as I raised a glass, "this party is on me!"

"Alice, that's crazy!" Peg protested.

"That's too much," Ilene chorused.

"What's put you in such a generous mood?" Laura asked. Had she thought I'd make a scene at Peg's party? Had she worried I'd publicly out her? Good.

"I'm happy today. Why shouldn't I spread it around?" I countered.

Laura excused herself and headed for the ladies room. We watched the back of her in silence.

"Come on, you two," I said as I straightened up in my chair and put my hands out to each of my friends.

This surprised Peg. "It's a little late to say grace, Alice. We've already eaten dessert."

"Think of this as my testimony," I said.

"What a sweet thing to do." Ilene put her hand in mine.

Peg did the same.

I might not have another chance to tell Peg and Ilene how grateful I was for their friendship. It had to be now. "I've spent nearly a decade putting my happiness on hold. But you've inspired me to believe it's time for a new season," I bared my heart to them. "I'm determined to be braver when I'm scared and more passionate even when it ties me in knots. Starting right now, I'm going to work like a monster and love like a fool."

"Good for you." Ilene squeezed my hand. "What kind of work? Do you mean work-work or self-realization work? Like *Eat, Pray, Love*? Alice, you're not going to Indonesia are you?"

"No, nothing like that," I said. It would be much further.

"Did you sign up for the writers' workshop at Adelphi? We'll carpool," Peg sounded so hopeful.

"I'm still exploring," I answered with a tug of guilt. "St. John's University has an excellent creative writing program. I've made an appointment to talk with their Graduate Arts and Sciences department tomorrow afternoon."

I wanted the attention off me before Laura returned from the rest room. My life was no longer her business. "Birthday girl," I continued, "there's a Korean expression that perfectly sums up how I feel about you. 'If only you were tiny, then I could put you in my pocket and take you everywhere I went.'" Maybe next year would find me driving to school with Peg or working with disenfranchised older women at the Korean American Charities Council or even scoping out publishers in both universes. I finally understood I had options that didn't depend on the color of the sky.

I stood up, shook the crumbs from my new linen skirt, kissed Peg's cheek, and signaled our waitress for the check.

Chapter

32: Daylight

The new lock on the kitchen door took two tries before I could open it. I hadn't expected Mike to sneak back in but I hired a locksmith anyway to make sure he couldn't. I had spent that afternoon going over my college transcript at St. John's. The fresh-faced associate dean with her little shirtdress and Birkenstock sandals looked young enough to be my daughter. She said I met the admissions requirements then asked me to send a copy of my college diploma.

I dropped the registration packet along with my purse and keys on the counter near the sink then slugged down a glass of cold water. Outside, blue spruce needles played rat-a-tat on the window boxes. I watched a pair of mourning doves bring twigs and leaves for their new nest. I knew I had a task to accomplish, just like the birds. After a deep breath, I went into Luke's and Will's bedroom.

I was pretty sure I had stored my diploma on the top shelf of the boys' closet. A folder peeked out from between the stored winter blankets, just reachable if I stood on my toes. It held my diploma and a pink envelope with two snapshots. One was of my boys and my parents on vacation. Luke and Will wore matching Amish straw hats, their arms wrapped around each other. *Twins and Grans—Lancaster Pa. 1982* was written on the back. My sons had been eight years old. My parents were younger than I was now.

The second photo was of Mike and the boys bringing in a tree for Christmas. Wasn't that the year Auntie bought them toy rockets?

I sat cross-legged on the carpeting next to the scorch mark from the time one of the rockets caught on fire. The rest of the rug had faded except for a suspicious stain in the corner that was probably Ginger's. The boys had often covered the dog's accidents with their book bags to protect her honor. I let the memories linger. Whether threadbare, scorched or soiled, this was holy ground to me. Could I really leave my sons' childhood home? What if Will and Ruthie came back from Africa and needed a place to stay? Shouldn't I remain here? Just in case? I had played the needed-mother card over and over in my head. The truth was Will would be too far away for me to drop by or for them to come back for holidays. Ruthie's parents hadn't returned to New York for twenty years. Will probably wouldn't either. Besides, twenty years plus my age…Will might have to visit me at the cemetery.

I scanned both sides of the Lancaster picture with my phone, slipped the original into my wallet, and returned the second photo to the envelope.

In my bedroom, I unzipped my skirt and wriggled free from my pantyhose till it landed on the floor like a curled kitten. Half undressed; I sat on the edge of the bed sorting my thoughts.

My approach to life had changed more since last August than the whole sixty-two years before. Instead of mourning Luke and worrying over Will, I now celebrated them. I had stopped surrounding myself with clutter from the past and had cleared a way for my future. I had become bold enough to apply for graduate school, and as soon as I could figure out the paperwork, I'd apply again in Red Sky.

Why hadn't I felt this way before? Maybe I was a late bloomer who needed two seasons to flower. It didn't matter. Red Sky had rescued me from my self-imposed exile. It was finally clear to me: Will didn't need this house and neither did I.

The scent of clean cotton linens on the bed invited me to lie down. It seemed decadent to be under the covers at three in the afternoon but what harm was there in resting my eyes?

As if it had been waiting for me, the image of the ill-fated *Palan Nun Aghesshi,* condemned to grow old long before her prince, filled my head. Where had I seen that portrait before? The top branches of the blue spruce tap-tapped my bedroom window. Tap-tap, it sounded again and again like talons on an herb shop counter …..*Mudang* Kim's shop! It was her face on his screen saver's laptop. How could that be? She never existed in this world. Except if…

I flew from the bed.

Mudang Kim didn't just sell the seeds, he took them! I bet that old scoundrel traveled back and forth and somehow, so did his electronics. And if that was true, then I could cross the universes and still stay in touch with Will.

I gulped down a packet of seeds and hopped back into bed.

무궁화

A fiery sky stretched above me as far as my eyes could see. My first daytime in Red Sky was too momentous to be filtered through the car's windshield. I pulled over to stand at the curb. The burnished heavens topped the neighborhood's lilac bushes and pansy beds. The red above me and the purple below was heady stuff indeed. It felt like I had stepped into a watercolor masterpiece.

I basked in the glorious colors before getting back into my car and joining the flow of traffic.

Right Turn Here! No moving motor vehicles in this Watch Zone till 12:00 a.m. First Watch 5-19-10. Time now: 5:32 p.m. Second Watch. No car horns or loud radios. Except for the Winkie-the-Bear turn sign at the intersection at Leeds Road and Little Neck Parkway, Red Sky's roadways at Second Watch looked very much like my day world in late afternoon. Please let the shop on Northern Boulevard be exactly where I last saw it.

무궁화

A free-standing greenhouse with a glittering *Herbz* sign marked the entry to Mr. Kim's store. I went inside. This time no soft sounds of wind chimes welcomed me. Instead, I was greeted by a throbbing K-Rock re-mix.

A twenty-something Asian man with diamond stud earrings stood behind a counter made from a surf board suspended from the ceiling by nylon ropes. His head tilted back to finish his Pepsi before crushing the can with his hand. His thumb and fingers were all long filed talons. *Mudang* Kim?

He lobbed the empty can into a basketball hoop above the back doorway. "Yes!" he yelled as the can dropped through the mesh.

To my right was a wall of blinking yellow, blue and green lights. A maze of glass blocks overhead scattered the colors like disco balls. It was hard to imagine this shop housed an ornate gilt cabinet with little fish drawer pulls in my other world. I thought about the first time I had met *Mudang* Kim right after my birthday dinner. My first night in Red Sky had un-nerved me so much, I had gone straight there the next morning to return the seeds. Now, after nearly a year of traveling, I felt at home in both my worlds.

He lowered the music and ducked under the counter to greet me.

"*Oh ren man ee yo*. Miss A," he welcomed.

"*Oh ren man ee yo*. Kim Ssi," I agreed. Long time, no see you too.

Young *Mudang* Kim led me to a makeshift sitting area fashioned from a pair of red stools and a mini-fridge freckled with travel magnets. "Let's take a load off," he pulled out one of the stools.

"I guess my visit doesn't surprise you," I said. But his new look sure surprised me. Joseph was right when he called *mudangs* screwy. Even thin-lipped Dr. Hong had said they were quite mad. "Do many of your customers find you in this world?" I asked.

"It happens," he said and took two cans of soda from the fridge. "Pepsi? It's better here. Beats me why."

"*Gam sah, Kim Ssi*," I thanked him.

"Rad impressive *Hangul*, Miss A. How'd you learn Korean so fast?" he asked before wiping down a can top with a corner of his tee shirt and handing it to me.

"I've been practicing," I answered. Late nights in bed with Hoon offering kisses for every Korean vocabulary word I learned was extremely motivating. "I have a question."

"*Aish*, more questions?" he whined like a pre-teen. "Want some *Seh-ooh Kkang?*" He held out an opened bag of shrimp chips.

"No thanks." I put my Pepsi on top of the mini fridge. "*Palan Nun Aghesshi…*"

He burped. The scent of cola and brine hung between us.

"*Kim Ssi,*" I continued. "After I saw *Palan Nun Aghesshi's* picture on your screen saver in our other world, I did a little research."

"I'm not permitted to speak of *Palan Nun Aghesshi* to other worlders," he tried to cut me off.

"I promise it's not about her. It's about *that.*" I pointed to his iPad on the counter. "I've figured out that electronics from one world can work in another. But they work independently. My cell works here but it can't call my house in Floral Park. Your tablet interfaces in two universes. You are able to connect your two worlds electronically. That's what I want to do." I stopped there. He didn't need to know this was about starting a life with Hoon without severing my ties with Will.

"Why didn't you say so? I can make that happen *anywhere*," the *mudang* poured the last crumbs of chips into his mouth. Clearly, being twenty six forever had made *mudang* Kim less inscrutable but totally obnoxious.

"Good, because this is important," I said as I got off the stool and stood over him. "*Kim Ssi*, I need you to make this happen."

"OK, OK. It's no biggie anyway. Take out your cell," he took the phone from me. "I'll download the app. This works with any device you have. First, go to social apps. See *Mujigeh?* It's Korean for rainbow. Get it? *Over* the rainbow? Wizard of Oz?" He laughed at his joke.

His talons clicked as he tapped *Accept and Download* on my cell. "This is your new home page. It does everything your old one did but wicked-more." He swiped his thumb across the screen. "This has all kinds of cool stuff. The WGPS is primo. Wait'll you see this."

"Does it have email?" I needed him to stay on task.

"That's a bit old school, Miss A, but sure. You can email, gmail, but no-no on the snail mail. Here, click on contacts," he instructed. "OK, E.T. Phone home." *If this doesn't work, my life here in Red Sky ends now.* I called Will.

"Hi Mom."

It was really Will.

"Mom?" Will repeated.

"I just called to say hi," I whispered into the phone and turned. I didn't want *Mudang* Kim seeing my eyes well up at the sound of my son's voice.

"Mom, I'm taking Top Tim the Burmese cat to radiology right now," Will said impatiently. "She tore her paw on a chain link fence. Can I call you back?"

"You can call me anytime," I said.

My heart was finally eased. Whatever the future held for us, Will could reach me in Red Sky.

Chapter

33: The First Wrinkle

After Hoon and I made love and opened a bottle of Barossa Valley Shiraz in the afterglow, he asked me to move in with him. Eleven years ago, when Luke announced he and Emma were going to live together, I had pleaded like Shakespeare's Portia for him to change his mind. They bought a condo in Bayside anyway.

"Move in?" I kissed Hoon's cheek. Guess he wasn't going to pop the M word. "You're such a romantic."

"I wish I could be. Don't you think I want to show up at your door with roses and a ring? But I don't know where you live. I'm scared you might be married or dying or even a damn *gu mi ho* after all. There's no end to what I think," he put his glass down on the night stand. The clink of glass on wood punctuated his words. "Marry me."

Had he just proposed? Oh, yes he did. I outlined his face with my fingertip. Hoon's black hair shimmered like spun silk in the lamp light. His leonine eyes looked back into mine. "Picture it, Alice," he said. "We'll wake up together in this bed. I'll make coffee. You can work on your novel out on the terrace."

"Can I catch the sunrise?" I asked. That would be the first thing I'd do.

"*Khrum.* Our apartment faces east," he pointed to the terrace doors. I wished I could have said yes and moved in right then. Could love conquer all after admitting I'm older than Disneyworld? "How can you be so sure we're meant to be together?" I asked.

"*Jah gi,*" Hoon kissed my forehead. "I'm Korean. I believe in three things: Rice is the staff of life, Korea's unification and *sarang eui gijeok,* the miracle of love. Can't you just say yes, Alice?"

The man who had launched the happiest time of my life just told me all I needed to know— love is a miracle. For as surely as I knew time would turn our hair silver and age lines would crisscross our faces, Hoon would still love me as if time hadn't changed us at all. I put my lips close to his ear and whispered, "Yes, yes, yes."

"All right! Let's update our status together," Hoon declared between kisses.

My brain was screaming orders—tell him. Tell him now! But we were so happy. I had to slow things down. "This isn't easy to explain but…," I started to say.

Hoon let go of me. "What isn't easy to explain?"

"We have to wait a little while," I back-pedaled.

Hoon pulled himself up to a sitting position. "How little is the while?"

I reached for my blouse on the nightstand as if sleeves and a collar could make me more authoritative. "I have to wrap up some things first," I said as I began buttoning up. "I love you, but…."

Hoon unbuttoned my blouse. "Don't say 'I love you *but*' ever again." He took my face in his hands. "Don't say anything."

Revelry sounded on Hoon's phone. It was Spencer. That man had such an uncanny ability to call whenever we were making love or just about to that Hoon had assigned him a separate ringtone. We thought it would make it easier to ignore his calls. But it hadn't worked out. Whenever we heard the ringtone, it felt like Spencer was climbing into bed with us.

"Jeez, Spenz," Hoon answered. "*Yeh, yeh.*" He nodded as he listened. I covered myself with the top sheet. Hoon tugged the sheet back. "Spenz is asking if we want to barbeque on July 4th?"

That was a month away. Leave it to Spencer to ask now. "Great,"

I said. I swung my legs to the side of the bed but Hoon pulled me back beside him. "Alice says great. We'll get back to you later."

He replaced his cell in its charger but something caught his eye and he took it back. He tapped the screen again.

"Another call?" I asked.

"No." Hoon got out of bed. "You know Spenz. He'll remember something else to say. I'll leave both phones in the kitchen." He took my cell from the bureau. "Be back in a flash."

What had just happened? A second ago, Hoon—my future husband, my intended, my fiancé—couldn't undress me fast enough. Now he was disappearing into the kitchen to check our cell phones.

"Let's catch a movie," he called over his bare shoulder. "I'll drive you home if it ends close to First Watch."

Something was definitely up. Not once since we met had I accepted his offer to drive me home. "We just killed a bottle of Shiraz. You shouldn't drive this Watch. The bus stops at my corner. I'll be fine," I insisted. Soon I wouldn't need any more excuses.

I gathered up my clothes and went to the bathroom. I caught myself frowning in the mirror. Is this how wrinkles begin, with the first worries? Why had Hoon offered to drive me home? He wasn't going to bring up where I lived again, was he? I turned on the shower. Why wouldn't he let it go? Will's wedding is only a few days away. When everything is settled and I'm free to spend my life here, I'll come clean. We'll sleep wrapped in each other's arms and wake up together in Red Sky.

Tendrils of steam sidled up to the mirror. I drew a circle with dot-eyes over my disappearing reflection. With any luck, I'd be ready to claim my new life and move in by Independence Day. I added a big smile to my drawing.

Chapter

34: Dreaming Big

All week long, the TV news predicted a scorcher on Saturday. By six that morning, the temperature had reached eighty. I texted Will: *Happy Wedding Day!* I headed for the bathroom but then I remembered another message I needed to send. *Happy Wedding Day!* I sent to my soon-to-be daughter-in-law.

In less than an hour, I had showered, made-up my face, and styled my hair. My phone rang just as I swished antiperspirant under my arms. Without my readers, I couldn't make out the name or number. "Hello."

"Alice." It was Mike. He better not ask me to invite Laura to the church.

"What is it?" I asked with the sharpest tone I could muster.

"Sorry to bother you but I left my cufflinks in my top drawer."

I had already emptied his dresser and boxed his things but I knew where to find them. "I'll bring them to the church. Bye-bye." I looked for the End Call button.

"Wait! I can get them now. I'm at the side door," he raised his voice. Why the heck didn't he ring the bell? But it was easy to guess why. After four decades of living in this house, he didn't want to ring the doorbell like a stranger. "Stay there," I said. "I'll be down when I'm dressed."

I took my time locating his cufflinks then stopped at the bathroom mirror to re-apply blush before heading downstairs.

My spandex body shaper made me long and lithe in my celadon sheath. Eat your heart out, Mike Pleasance, I told my image.

He took his cufflinks from me and dropped them in his pocket. Over the years, I had fastened them for him more times than I could count but he was on his own now. I looked at the oven clock. Mike noticed. "Do you have a minute?" he asked.

On our son's wedding day? Still, he may finally offer his long-overdue apology for screwing the neighbor-lady who could have poisoned me with those seeds. "If it doesn't take long," I said.

Mike tugged up on his collar. He'd been self-conscious about his double chin since college. "I wanted you to know that you were always a great wife and a super mother. *And* beautiful. What happened with me and Laura wasn't because of you...."

This wasn't an apology. He was working up to an explanation and I didn't need to hear it. "Mike, I have things to do," I said as I shuffled him out the door.

무궁화

The June sun bleached its territory white on the crisp blue sky. Neighborhood linden blossoms perfumed the air. I took out my cell phone to photograph the Grace Church welcoming sign. *This is your Father's house, please feel at home. 10 a.m. nuptials of Ruth Jeanne Cole and William David Pleasance.*

I kept my wrap around my shoulders to hide any perspiration half-moons that might have seeped through.

"Hey, gorgeous!" Peg called out from across the street. She and Ilene left their husbands on the sidewalk to hug me.

"Kisses for the new mother-in-law," Peg said as her cheek clung to mine.

"From me too." Ilene squeezed between us. We were sticky from three shades of melting make-up. They'd never know that my dewiness was mixed with goodbye tears for their thirty years of friendship.

Unlike my modern church, Grace Church had a nearly two-hundred year old history. Unfortunately, it had just begun its expansion project. Black netted scaffolding covered most of its aged clapboard siding. Ruthie's cousin, who was the unofficial photographer, asked the bridal party to hurry inside for pictures.

Most of the guests followed her command. Auntie's health aide nimbly guided her wheelchair up a make-shift ramp. "Alice," Auntie called to me, "why are the children getting married in a bombed out church?" She squinted behind her glasses. "Looks like London after the Blitz."

"The war's over, Auntie," I said. "We won." I straightened her corsage. "Let's get you a front row seat."

"There's my favorite girl," Mike said as he rose from the first pew to greet his aunt. Auntie adjusted her glasses for a better look at him.

"Our William has the same high forehead as Michael," she said. She was right. He did. "Alice, did I tell you Will and Ruthie stopped in at my flat last week," she daubed the sweat from her brow with a hankie. "She's a lovely girl. She'll be good for Will."

"Yes, Auntie," I agreed. The old gal could be a darling when she was lucid.

Mike walked up the aisle to maneuver her wheelchair into the groom's row. After tucking her chair up against the pew, he patiently helped her pull on her lace gloves. Even if Mike had only visited Auntie a tenth of the times he claimed, he was still a loving nephew.

I checked the time on my phone. In less than eight hours, Will and Ruthie would be on their way to Dar Es Salam. I needed one more mom-hug and enough time to tell him how much I loved him.

"Will, can you spare a second?" I asked. This was his wedding day, I knew he couldn't but I led him out of the chapel anyway. The small vestibule next to the church kitchen was rumored to be the last stop to freedom on the Underground Railroad before the Civil War. It was the perfect setting to offer Will his emancipation from me.

"Will." I took his face in my hands.

"Mom," he said as he eased my hands away, "you're not going to get all weepy, are you?"

"I'm not going to cry," I promised. What a senseless thing to say. Will was looking right at my waterworks. I ran a dampened tissue over my cheek. Thirty five years ago, I gave birth to two sons. I buried the oldest. How could I let go of Will? "I wanted to tell you something that you'll always remember. I just don't know what that should be."

He tapped his fingers on his knee. The biggest celebration in his life was about to start in the next room, and I was keeping him from joining in.

"Will," I hesitated. The happy voices outside quieted in expectation.

"William David," I said. The organ was going to sound any second. "You knew Ruthie was the girl for you and you didn't let anything stand in your way. And while most people are scared to move across town, you're getting ready to live on the other side of the world. Pretty soon you'll be eye to eye with African elephants. You don't need parting advice from me." I drank in every detail of his face. "Just keep dreaming big."

35: Seventy times Seven

I was teetering on a step stool emptying out the china cabinet. Outside, giant sycamores behind the Novak's house all but hid the eastern horizon. It was only when a breeze set the treetops quivering that the sun's blinding shrapnel disrupted my work. I remembered seven years ago cleaning out my mother's house after she passed. I had packed up everything my basement could hold and those boxes were still waiting to be unwrapped. Holding onto things had stifled rather than sheltered me.

I climbed down to close the blinds. Jeanette Novak was weeding the berry patch around her evergreens. Were her strawberries ripe already? The last time I saw Jeannette in her front yard was when she and her children were making a snowman. That was the day Mike and I had the snowball fight. He had pulled me to the ground and I wondered if he'd kiss me. Then Laura made that nasty comment from her window. Was that only a season ago?

Jeanette stopped to adjust the band on her baseball cap.

"Hi, neighbor," I called from the front door.

She stopped her work to wave. "Hi, Alice, how was the wedding?"

"Beautiful. You'll have three of your own before you know it. Do you have time for coffee?" I asked.

She dropped her gardening gloves into the plant tray. "I'd love a break."

Inside, she slipped off her muddy sneakers in the front hall and stepped over a tray of crystal sherry glasses to get to the dining room.

"Are you moving?" she surveyed the rug, cardboard boxes and reams of bubble wrap; the vestiges of things left behind.

"More like moving on," I said.

Jeanette let her gaze linger on a china cup. "My mother-in-law had Lenox too. Your pattern is even prettier. It's called Eternal. Right?"

"Yes, it's Eternal," I said. Although nothing but heaven ever is. "Service for twelve…and I have the serving pieces as well." I cleared paper from a chair for her and brought in our pot of coffee.

"Smells great. Thanks." Jeanette had pulled off her cap, letting her chestnut hair fall to her shoulders.

"Mike and I have separated," I said. Maybe I should have softened that a bit. Like, oh, by the way.

"I'm sorry. Do you think you'll get back together?" she asked.

"As soon as Porky and Miss Piggy fly," I said and nudged the sugar bowl towards her.

"At least you kept your sense of humor," she said while pouring half the little pitcher of skim milk into her cup. "I was divorced before I met Matt. I sure didn't joke about it. At the time, I was about as funny as crabgrass."

I topped up Jeanette's cup with coffee. I wished I had cake to offer.

"My older brother helped me work through my pain," she divulged. "He heard me screaming like a banshee at our Mom one day. He knew it wasn't the first time I had lost control over something stupid." She added a heaping spoonful of sugar to her cup. "He led me out to his car for a private intervention."

"It must be wonderful to have a big brother," I said.

"I have a mega-big brother. Mark is six-four and over two hundred pounds. I got into the backseat of his Chevy like a little lamb." She chuckled over her recollection.

"What did he do?" I asked.

"He closed the car windows and told me to keep all my anger inside," she said.

That hardly seemed enough to change a life

"Then he pointed out I could hold a grudge forever," she lifted her cup with both hands.

That was true of me as well. I was pretty sure I could hate Mike and Laura until kingdom come.

"And then?"

"And then he made me sit with him in that closed car," she said after her slog of milky coffee.

"For how long?" *Was her brother a psycho?*

"Until we sucked up all the air. We were covered in sweat and I demanded he open the doors. That's when Mark really let me have it. He blasted me, curse words and all. 'You want to be free from that prick? Forgive him. Right now and every day. Otherwise you'll be gasping for breath the rest of your life,'" she imitated a gruff voice.

Could I forgive Mike? Weren't there as many happy times with him as horrible ones? The last time I had set this table with my good dishes was the Easter Sunday before Luke was killed. I was taking the string bean casserole from the oven when Will challenged Mike and Luke to a clean plate contest.

"You're on," Mike started the count down, "three, two, one." With Auntie, Luke's Emma, and my Mom cheering them on, they scarfed down ham with mashed potatoes and gravy. By the time I brought in the vegetables, they were licking their plates to a shine. Mike had gravy on his forehead and Emma had caught Will hiding ham slices under the table. We kept laughing all through Easter dinner.

"Would you like this set?" I held up the gravy boat. "You mentioned you were fond of the pattern."

Would she think I was crazy? A full service of Lenox dishes was easily worth three thousand dollars and Jeanette and I weren't really friends. A fast hello and goodbye as we went on with our lives were as close as New York City neighbors got. Jeanette picked at a thread on the brim of her cap. I was pleased she didn't jump at my offer. My china may have been just bits of pottery but I wanted them in a good home.

"Alice, don't you think you'll use them again?" she asked.

"My mother bought them for me when I got engaged. I stopped having formal holiday dinners years ago," I explained. "They're just dust collectors now."

"Doesn't your new daughter-in-law want them?" she asked.

"Ruthie and Will are in Africa. They're part of a long-term mission in Moshi. You'd really be helping me if you took them," I placed the soup tureen in front of her.

"I don't know what to say." Her eyes took in its impressive size, "I never thought I'd own something as beautiful as this."

We wrapped the pieces in linen napkins and cushioned them with tablecloths. After we carried the boxes across to her house, Jeanette thanked me with a jar of her homemade strawberry jam. She filled her kitchen sink with dish liquid and warm water then gently lowered the soup tureen into the froth. "I'll take good care of it...every single piece," she promised.

She swabbed the inside of the tureen with a soapy sponge. It brightened for its new owner.

Chapter

36: Forgiveness

The bedroom was stifling. I kicked off my top sheet and wiped the perspiration from my neck. For more Junes than I cared to count, I had to beg Mike to put in the window air conditioners but he rarely got around to the chore until mid-July. Now it was my job, and just the thought of starting the day by hauling out the dolly and power drill made me appreciate Mike's yearly reluctance. It would have to wait until I finished cleaning. I went downstairs in my pajamas.

Sweltering or not, I was determined to empty the hall closet. My mother's mink stole, the one I swore I'd remake into a vest one day, was put into a carton for the church thrift shop. It was followed by four folding umbrellas and an assortment of knit hats and scarves. Mike's belongings filled the biggest box. Thirty-eight years of Old Spice cologne wafted off his wool coats and down jacket. Even his old bowling bag testified that its owner was Luke's and Will's father and my husband.

After sealing the cartons, I showered, dressed, and texted Mike to stop by.

An hour later, with Mike's help, the window air-conditioners sputtered into action. He loaded the box of his winter clothes into his car trunk and when he came back inside, we split a Diet Sprite and bag of Goldfish crackers.

Mike wrapped his thumb with a paper napkin.

"Did you get hurt?" I asked.

"I must have cut myself on one of the window frames." He put his hand on his lap. "Are you moving away?"

Soon I'd be so far away that there wasn't even the remotest chance that I'd ever see Mike again. I wanted to scream at him, "you and Laura thought you'd be the ones who were going," but kept my thoughts to myself.

He stared at me. He had spent four decades deciphering my expressions so there was no point in refusing to answer.

"Yes, I'm going away," I said. But I was packing light—a ruby ring on my finger, Hoon's gold band in a box, and treasured photos on my phone. I didn't even need a nightie.

"Can you ship those things there?" He pointed to a double stack of cartons.

It was finally out in the open. When Mike and Laura realized she couldn't go to Red Sky, they deported me. He had witnessed my transformation while pretending to be asleep and kept up the charade throughout the winter, even when I grew too weak to get out of bed.

"You're worried about shipping? How could you let me morph into someone else and walk out the door in the middle of the night?" I spat my words like venom.

"For God's sake, Alice, it wasn't banishment," he lobbed back. "When the seeds didn't work for Laura, she came up with the idea to send you."

I bet she did.

"She said the seeds would help you find Luke in the other universe. You'd be with him and I'd get to stay here with Will," he rationalized. "This whole thing was supposed to be good for all of us. And I swear, when the seeds made you sick, I was going to stop....," he hesitated. "Anyway, after a while, you were healthier. Really. And happier than for as long as I could remember."

I turned my ruby ring around my finger and thought of who I was before last August—a pathetic victim who was sure my best days were on the road behind me. I stuffed the balled up cracker bag into my empty glass.

"I thought it was a win-win, Alice," he insisted.

Mike was right. It was a win-win. We had trudged through the same hellish nightmare together yet managed to find our own separate peace. In Red Sky, I learned to welcome every precious moment. This *had* been my winning season. Hoon and I were happy. If Mike and Laura were happy too, it wouldn't diminish my joy. Besides, no matter what, he was Will's father. He's been there for him at every game, graduation and personal goal. Still, I had to be sure Will could rely on his Dad.

"We weren't always in sync when we raised the boys but they knew if one parent wasn't around they could always count on…." I started to say.

"We're still a team Alice, even if you go away," he finished my thought.

"Promise me he can count on you."

"Alice, I would never have taken all the money," he vowed as he adjusted his makeshift bandage. "I haven't been the best parent but I love our son." Mike blotted the growing circle of blood on his thumb. "Will told me there are short-term missions in Moshi every spring. I got the forms to go next year. We'll both benefit from a little father-son bonding."

"Will would love that," I said. That was blessed assurance to my ears. "I have something to give you." I left the table.

When I returned, I handed Mike the extra house key from the locksmith. "Don't unpack your boxes yet. This house is still yours. I'll let you know when I'm leaving."

He stared at the shiny key in his palm. "There's something I want you to know. In the beginning… I really believed you found Luke over there."

"How could you think that? Wouldn't I have told you? He was our son," I jumped on his words.

"Please let me finish." Mike's pale eyes filled with tears. "I need to hear you say it. He's not in the place you go, is he?"

"Luke was only here with us." I draped my arms around his neck. "Now he's with God." Finally, my tears came. Why hadn't we mourned together before? It didn't matter. Life cannot be undone.

We stepped away from each other.

"I'll get a Band-Aid for you," I said and headed for the pantry closet. "Mike, do we still have the first aid kit we bought at Costco?"

"Look behind the drain-opener," he called back.

I bandaged his thumb before sending him off.

Chapter

37: Mercy and Justice

That July, the east coast humidity oozed through the walls, turning my bedroom into an orchid hothouse. I braved a cold shower to cool myself down before the heat of the day. The chain on the silver cross Will had given me for my last birthday had tangled in my wet hair. I put on my readers to unsnag it.

One Christmas when the twins were little, my parents gave them gold crosses. Luke had been hinting for a train set and couldn't hide his disappointment but Will was eager to have the cross lie on his heart. "Look, Mom, I got my God on," he would say. *You certainly do, my darling.*

Downstairs, I put up coffee and wrote till noon. My regimen of ten pages of *Blue Skies* each day since February had produced half a manuscript. Even though it was autobiographical, I'd have to market it as science fiction. Who would believe a tale of magic seeds, *mudangs* and bi-universal phone apps? I wondered if Ray Bradbury also experienced the things he wrote about.

Writing done for the day, I called Hoon but was routed to his voice mail. It was the third time this week. I knew he was on a business trip but no time to talk at all? I checked the time. It was 12:32 p.m. Second Watch. Hoon was due back any minute…probably texting right now. Or was he still angry with me?

"When do you want to introduce me to your family?" he had asked over dinner the night before his trip.

"Soon." I twirled my pasta with my fork. "There're still things I need to finish up."

"I don't like the sound of that, Alice," he shook his head no.

My plan was to wait until I was safely ensconced in Red Sky before making my confession to Hoon. It was a selfish decision born of the fear of losing him. "Pretty soon." I mumbled. How lame did that sound?

"Soon? Like in I'll say *soon* to get my boyfriend off my back," he pushed his plate away.

"I don't know what more I can say, Hoon."

"I've got my first road trip for my job next Watch," he said and left the dinner table. "I'll be out of town till Friday."

We hadn't skipped three Watches together since we began dating. I missed him so much. Why don't I text him at work? I hit my *Mujigeh* app and began,. R U BZ? Want to meet @ 7:PM SW?

An opened bottle of pinot grigio and a half carton of eggs were the only things keeping each other company on my refrigerator's shelf. My groceries, like my life, reflected my single status. I made scrambled eggs and checked my phone. Chrissy had forwarded an e-vite from Asian American Women in Business. The summer's charity event would be at the Midtown Terrace on 5th Avenue. Had it been almost a year since Chrissy brought me to Fendi for free champagne? There were no messages from Hoon.

While I washed down my eggs with wine, I sent an email to Will and Ruthie in Moshi. They'd been gone five days but had only sent a quick message when they arrived. It was time to be a mother-in-law. Miss you both so much, I wrote.

By early afternoon, the sky had turned watery blue. I loaded two cartons of clothing for my church's thrift shop into my back seat, aimed the car vents at my face, and turned the air conditioner on high. Goose bumps dappled my arms by the time I merged onto Little Neck Parkway.

Construction workers were putting down road cones. A few cars were ushered through. I followed. Then a sinewy road worker in a hardhat labeled *Kyle N.* in reflective tape motioned for me to stop. "Didn't you see my flag go up, ma'am?"

"What?"

"We're repairing the divider. You gotta take this turn," he shouted over the traffic noise.

I detoured to Browvale Lane looking for a shortcut, but it too was closed off for construction. After facing a dead end, I pulled over to engage my phone's GPS. The screen turned red—be advised WGPS in use! I hadn't seen that before. Had the new *Mujigeh* app screwed up my navigator? The screen returned the map with a recording: "Recalibrating."

So was I.

It took several back streets with gaping pot holes and mountainous school-crossing bumps to finally arrive at St. Andrew's parking lot. Another car pulled up beside mine. A black woman with a heavy island accent was shouting into her cell phone and unbuckling her toddler from his car seat. They disappeared into the church.

I heard the crackling of tires on gravel again as a beige Ford Escape came up the drive. I remembered when Pastor Morgan bought that car. I could even recall the old Chevy he drove when he'd first arrived at St. Andrew's. He had known me fifteen years, the Alice before Luke's death and the Alice after.

I opened the passenger door and started unloading my cartons onto the walkway. Goodbye Christmas cardigans and Easy Spirit loafers. Enjoy your new lives.

"Let me give you a hand," Pastor Morgan said as he helped me carry my donations to the basement thrift shop. As portly as he was, my pastor was still ten years my junior with a servant's heart: the job was finished in no time.

"Anything else, Alice?" he asked.

"Actually, I came to have a talk with you, Pastor. Can you spare a few minutes?"

"Of course, but I'm hearing the fellowship kitchen's pudding cups calling my name. Care to join me?" he invited.

"Yes, please." I followed him up the stairs.

He pulled a metal tray of puddings, spoons and napkins from the refrigerator. "Nothing goes better with a talk than snacks," he said. We headed for his office.

I held the tray while he unlocked the door. Last Easter, I had described my travels as a plot for a short story. It was time for a more direct talk, although not a detailed one. And absolutely no more lies.

Pastor Morgan opened his office window, brushed pretzel crumbs from his desk then squeezed into his chair. "By the abundance of your donation, I'll guess you're having quite a clean-out," he fished.

"Actually, I'll be traveling soon but I wanted to touch base with you first," I said.

"Yes, yes, of course, with Will married and doing God's work, you're footloose and fancy-free again. Parenthood flies. My eldest turns twelve this year. Before I know it, she'll be off on her own, and that's how it should be," he said wistfully.

Was it? If Mike and Peg and now my pastor were so convinced Will would be fine without me, why wasn't I?

Pastor Morgan took one of the spoons off the tray. "So Alice, where are you going?"

I hadn't planned for that question. If I started with a sin of omission, how could I enter Red Sky with clean hands and pure heart? Lord, I'm so sorry. Please fill me up and send me out anyway.

"I've decided to begin again," I was amazed at the strength of my voice.

There was a soft double tap on the opened door. A church elder holding a large accounts ledger took two steps inside the office. "Excuse me Pastor, where are we supposed to find funds for the Mercy and Justice Ministry this month? You cut a check for the Angel Orphanage without telling us."

"Stop me if you've heard this before, Robbie," Pastor Morgan said. "As you did not do it to one of the least of these, you did not do it to me."

"Duly noted, Pastor… this time," the elder had more to say. "Do I have your promise you'll curb your generosity until next quarter?"

Pastor Morgan offered the look that he usually saved for petulant teens at our church's youth group. The elder closed the ledger. "I'll guess we'll find it somewhere, Pastor," he sighed. He kept the door ajar when he left.

"Chocolate or vanilla?" Pastor Morgan held up two cups. "God's children renew themselves all the time, Alice. This isn't for permission, is it?" I knew he preferred chocolate so I took the vanilla cup.

"This place I have found, Pastor, at first it was simply my time-out, a haven from the place where I was dead inside." I peeled the foil liner off the pudding. "But now, I want to live again and put down roots. That's OK, isn't it?"

He used his spoon as a pointer. "How many Sundays have you heard Assurances of Pardon. 'The old life is gone; a new life has begun.' Of course, that doesn't mean we do anything we feel like. We must keep trying to do good works until heaven comes down. I believe you will put down roots by finding your purpose," he said as he settled back in his chair and dug his spoon into the cup. "Alice, by God's grace, you survived a tragic and terrible season. Go. Let your new life begin. Who knows? Your purpose may very well find you."

I allowed myself a last fill of his face. Pastor Morgan's sharp green eyes and chubby cheeks made him look more like a clean-shaven Santa than good shepherd. Still, as surely as he believed the church would find the means for the little ones at Angel Orphanage, he also had faith that Will would make his way in this world, and I could make my way in mine. I was truly going. In a short while, I'd eat those seeds for the last time, sleep deeply and peacefully in Red Sky and wake up to a sunrise that I had only seen in my imagination. Hoon and I would grow old together in the fullness of time and Will could talk to me whenever he liked. How should one react when a dream comes true? I chose to finish my pudding.

The desk phone rang. "I'll let you get on with your work, Pastor," I rose from my chair.

He told the caller to hold. "Let me see you out, Alice."

He stopped in the doorway and took my hands in his. Does he realize this is our last time together? Undoubtedly.

"When will you be leaving?" he asked.

I wanted to spare us both a teary goodbye. "I don't have an exact date yet."

"You called your past the place where you were dead inside. Reflect on *Ephesians*, Alice. 'Awake O sleeper, and arise from the dead….'"

Chapter

38: Chrysalis

I checked my cell in the church parking lot—7 p.m. was hours away. There was still no message from Hoon but Chrissy had texted again:

Wanna DD FW??

DD? I had to stop and think. Double date. I texted back: Can't do FW.

I got into my car. Chrissy would ask why. I'd better shoot off another text. H back frm Bz trip;)—tmrw?? The smiley wink would say Hoon and I wanted to be alone. That's what I wanted. I certainly hoped he did too.

Even before our last Watch together, Hoon seemed distracted. I shouldn't be over-analyzing what was likely just new job jitters. I stayed in my parked car to plan his welcome home. After a bite together, I'd send Hoon back to work, shop for wine and nibbles and wait at his place, soon to be my place. I checked my phone for local wine shops. The darn WGPS warning wouldn't shut off. Hoon would know how to fix it.

The church bus pulled up beside me. Should Hoon and I make love first or start with wine? Wine, definitely…on the couch. He could lay his head on my lap while I massaged his brow and told him everything: How I got to Red Sky and why I'd never leave.

I re-texted. Rmber, u & me alone @ 7:SW.

What if I never told him? Once I slept in Red Sky, I'd become just another twenty-six year old. Hoon wouldn't know. No one would know.

I started the car and adjusted my rear-view mirror. I would know. Maybe I hadn't the courage before but I was going to tell Hoon everything today. I'd been the victim of secrets and I knew the anguish of being betrayed. I wouldn't deceive Hoon for another second.

While I was at the church, the afternoon sun continued baking the house. *I should have left an air conditioner on. I won't be here when the utilities bill arrives anyway. Mike's moving back as soon as I leave. He can pay it.* I picked up the mail at the front door and left it on the kitchen table. When was the last time I soaked in a tub?

Attar of roses bath oil soothed my tired back and aching knees. I wouldn't miss this body any more than a butterfly would long for its chrysalis.

Mike's shaving mirror still hung from the shower head. I took in the face I wouldn't see again for many years. *Listen to me old girl,* I told myself. *When we meet again, you better be twice as smart and seriously committed to daily exercise. Maybe I should cut out sugar and white flour from my diet while I'm young. Nah.* I dunked my head under the water then popped back up. What time was it? Hoon should have called back by now.

My phone buzzed from the shelf. *Hoon?* I stood dripping to reach it. "Free T-Mobile Msg," it read. My bill was due. Where was Hoon? I scrolled down the logs. No calls. No texts. He hadn't been in touch with me in three Watches. This wasn't a business trip. I pulled the stopper from the tub.

Why was I so stupid? Hoon's new job was the same as Mike's Auntie—an excuse. He'd been sending cryptic signals since I asked him to wait for me. We hadn't made love in a week. Why hadn't I questioned him? I thought I'd learned to stand up for myself, not shrink as I did when Mike was cheating. Yet there I was, once again sopping wet in the bathroom trying to figure things out.

I was still damp from my bath when I went downstairs. Bits of cardboard and wrapping paper left on the carpet stuck to my bare feet. Maybe a little cleaning-therapy would burn off my negative energy. I dragged the vacuum cleaner through the living room then mopped the kitchen floor.

Mike and I had put down the linoleum tiles ourselves the week we moved in. My parents came to help. "It's broom-clean, Alice," Mom had said. "That'll bring you good luck." In the most profound way it had. I was ready to meet my future. I hoped Hoon would be too. The house phone rang. I let the answering machine take the call.

One by one I surveyed the rooms of my little house. From the basement laundry room to the unfinished attic and all the spaces between, the chronicles of my family followed me. I lingered a while in the boys' room but eventually closed their door behind me.

These things I knew were true: Hoon wasn't Mike and I wasn't the old Alice. Whatever problems were afoot, Hoon and I would face them together.

무궁화

The feathery lilac mist outside the kitchen door cleared, as it always did, by the time I'd driven past the first cross street and entered Red Sky. Hoon's new office was more than a mile from the Rapid Eastern Metro bus stop. I'd have to take the railroad to be at his building before Lunchtime: Second Watch ended.

Within minutes after the train pulled into Penn Station, I was entering Hoon's building. It was the first time I had been inside. Men and women smelling of cigarettes and lunch rushed to the elevators. I called Hoon from the lobby.

"I'm at the front desk. Let's talk," I said in my message then took a seat on the leather ottoman opposite a notice that read *Guests Must Sign In.* The run from Penn Station had heated my cheeks. I swept my hair off my neck to cool down.

The concierge, his greasy sideburns combed into two points at his chin, kept me in his sights while he signed for packages and answered the phones. He had no sooner hung up when another one rang. "Main Desk, Roman speaking."

He looked up. "Excuse me." His gold front tooth glinted when he spoke. "Are you Alice?"

"Yes." I jumped to my feet.

"Mr. Park isn't available," he said and quickly hung up to greet a busty woman in a skimpy sundress.

무궁화

Seventh Avenue swallowed me up. It wasn't till I reached the sculpture of the Garment Worker at 39th street that I escaped the crowds. I stopped to think under the big bronze sewing machine. Was that our break-up? Mr. Park isn't available? Right after his proposal? Blood pounded inside my elbows and wrists. Text me please, I pleaded in silence. Say anything. I clutched my cell phone so tightly, it shut off. I squeezed the button till the screen re-lit: Be advised WGPS in use!

Mudang Kim's app had definitely screwed up my service. I pushed down hard on every icon. Be advised WGPS in use! Be advised WGPS in use! Oh, shut up.

The foot traffic was building again as the next Second Watch lunch hour began. A young woman, her luminous pink hair chopped to the quick behind her ear, stopped to take pictures. "Would you mind staying still for a sec? I need a picture of the old guy at his sewing machine for a project," she said.

"I'll get out of your way," I said as I rose to leave.

"No. I want you in the frame. I like the juxtaposition of the tired old man lost in his thoughts and you lost in yours." She captured me in her lens. "Don't smile. OK?"

I had nothing to smile about.

Click, click. Her camera looked expensive and complicated. She circled to my right, adjusted something, turned something else and clicked again.

"Excuse me." I held up my phone to show the signal. "Do you know anything about the WGPS on cell phones?"

"I'm a total techno-geek. Did your WGPS stop working?" she asked and sat beside me on the sculpture base to check my phone.

"It's working. See, you're getting the warning now," she pointed to the irritating message.

"What does that mean?"

"Someone is tracking you," she said.

"You mean here, right now?"

"Yeah, the warning only goes on if it's someone other than Homeland Security. No biggie. Just enter your number in this box and hit *Unavailable*. Want me to show you?" she asked.

"No thanks, I'm OK," I said. But I wasn't. The *Mujigeh* app had turned my phone into a Red Sky phone complete with tracking device. Could Hoon locate me at home? If the old me doesn't exist here, who's at my house? Does my house exist here? It doesn't matter. Whatever he finds, he'll know I'm a liar.

The photographer waved goodbye and left.

How long has he known? I wondered. Last winter, Hoon said he couldn't locate me on the WATCH GPS which made sense because I didn't have a *Mujigeh* app yet. But when *Mudang* Kim installed it, my two worlds became linked turning on the WGPS.

I let out a groan. Of course, the night he proposed. His phone signaled my location at his address. That's why he took the phones to the kitchen. And why he offered to drive me home. I started trembling. I didn't want him to find out about me this way.

The sun dipped behind Broadway leaving the day's sweltering heat behind. I stayed seated on the bronze base. The afternoon I caught Mike lying had made me sick and yet I had kept up my own charade. Why hadn't I told Hoon my real story sooner? What a sad comical fate: I lied to keep him and lost him because I lied.

I sent Hoon another text.

Please. You know where I am. I'll wait here.

39: *Sarang Eui Gijeok,* The Miracle of Love

Hoon did not come.

I headed back to Queens. The 10:31 p.m.-SW train to Little Neck Station roared through the Midtown tunnel, pitching its cars into darkness. Overhead, the lights flickered before brightening. My WGPS signal remained constant. Was Hoon tracking me until he was sure I was back in my world and out of his life forever?

The train climbed out of its East River cocoon. The conductor spoke through the speakers as we slowed to a stop: "Woodside Station. Mind the gap."

We started again. Through my window, the street lights lit up in uniform grids like stars in a universe created by mathematicians. If only I could tell Hoon everything now, he'd understand.

"Auburndale Station."

A teenager in a grimy tee shirt and dragging his scuffed book bag took the empty seat beside me. I tried to concentrate on the night landscape while he whined into his phone. "I'm sorry, Ma. I was gonna hang out for an hour but they needed one more guy for b-ball. I'm on my way home right now. Call me back when you get this message."

He reeked of perspiration and pubescence, scents I recognized from raising two boys. He was probably telling his mom the truth.

She must have been worried sick, the poor dear. Well, at least he left a voice mail.

"Next stop, Bayside Station."

Even if Hoon wouldn't speak to me, I could still come clean by voice mail. I found a different seat at the back of the car and called.

"I'm sorry…for the things I didn't say." *Please listen, please.* "I've traveled from a parallel universe." *That sounds so crazy.* "I was born in 1947. I grew up in Queens. When I was in elementary school, the Korean War broke out. We wore dog tags and our teacher taught us to duck for cover in case there was a bombing. The 1950s for me isn't a chapter in a history book. It's my childhood." *This was what I should have told him months ago. Was it too late?* I kept talking.

"I preferred playing dress-up to riding bikes. Mostly, I liked to read. My parents said, 'Our Alice never complains or fusses.' It was the way I moved through life, hardly making a ripple."

A long bell tone signaled my message time had ended. I called again. "I've been a Mets fan since April 17th, 1964 when my Dad took me to opening day at Shea. We lost to Pittsburg. I was a bridesmaid at my cousin Susan's wedding when Neil Armstrong landed on the moon. The whole bridal party left her reception to watch it on TV at a local bar."

The train rumbled into northeastern Queens. "I had a major crush on Paul McCartney and cried when he married Linda Eastman." *What else? What else?* "Somewhere in my attic are pictures of me in bellbottoms and love beads." *That's not important. Think.* "I always wanted to be a writer but until I met you, I had put my dream aside."

The train slowed to a stop. "Bayside Station. If you see something, say something," the conductor called out.

"I married after college. That's over now. My twins, Luke and Will, were born seven minutes apart." I stopped. Could I speak about my sons without choking up? "Will has Asperger's syndrome. He's grown into a fine man. He and his wife are missionaries in Africa. Luke was a police officer assigned to the One Three in Midtown. He was killed on 9/11." I couldn't stem the flood of tears. "I wouldn't allow myself to recall any happy memories of him…until I fell in love with you." I ended the call to weep into my tissue. It wasn't just for Luke.

Douglaston Station flew by. "Next stop Little Neck," crackled though the speakers.

I redialed. "My sky comes in a thousand shades of blue. I bought an aquamarine ring so you could see. I'm sorry I put off giving it to you." Hoon would have had something to remember me by. If he wanted to remember me at all.

"I don't know exactly how I ended up in Red Sky, the name I call your world. Most of the things here are still a mystery to me," I blotted my nose with the last of my tissues.

The train had already passed the Manor. In less than a minute, I'd be back in Little Neck. *What if he's deleting my messages?* "Hoon, There's so much more I need to tell you but at least you know the me before you." I held my phone between my chin and shoulder to take my car keys from my bag.

"As for who I am now, I still slam doors when I'm angry, sulk when I'm sad and not a day goes by when I don't sweat the small stuff. I can't promise those things will change but I swear I'm not a *gweeshin* or *gumiho*, or the girl from a Joseon folk tale. I'm Alice, not new or improved, just Alice, again."

"Little Neck Station. Remember your belongings."

무궁화

Detour signs at Little Neck Parkway and Northern Boulevard sent me several streets out of my way, but eventually led me to Winkie the Bear's billboard across from the Rapid Eastern Metro bus stop and back into the violet haze.

Red and blue eddies born of rain and dew circled me when I got out of my car. Should I wait here a little longer? Hoon still might call. My cell phone darkened. The WGPS signal was gone. He had stopped looking for me. Even the Blue Eyed Girl's prince had loved her enough to see her off.

At the far end of the street, a car's head lights broke through the mist then extinguished. I waited in the driveway. Just in case. There was a thud as a car door slammed. Then the stillness returned. I climbed the stairs to unlock my door.

"*Kah ji mah!* Don't leave, *jeh bahl*. Alice please don't leave."

"Hoon!" I left the key dangling from the lock, ran down the steps and across a half dozen front lawns to him.

"Stay with me," his arms wrapped around me.

Hoon and I stood as one in the mist. I breathed him in. *This is real. This is real.* "I'm sorry I didn't tell you about my traveling from the start. I was afraid you'd leave...."

"It's OK. We're OK. I probably wouldn't have believed you. It's better that I found out myself," he whispered in my ear.

I took a step back. How long had he known? "The WGPS?" I asked.

"The night I proposed, your cell signaled you were at my place. When you left, it led me right to this spot," he stroked my cheek with the back of his hand.

He's known for weeks?

"I watched you, right over there in that empty lot." Hoon pointed at my house. "You walked up into the clouds like you were climbing upstairs. Just like tonight. And then you disappeared. It scared the hell out of me. I had to track down your friend, the one you called the leading authority on parallel universes," he shook his head at the absurdity of it all.

"You talked to Joseph?"

"He did most of the talking." Hoon took his keys from his pocket. "When he finally convinced me you really were from another world, I went down to K-Town and got Wakie-mad drunk."

My heart pounded inside me. What was he saying?

Hoon pressed his car key. The horn belched two times. Was he leaving? Was this I love you but seriously, you're old enough to be my gran?

"By Second Watch, and with the worst hangover in recorded history, it hit me: The woman I love moved heaven and earth just to be with me," he tilted my chin to look into my eyes. "I really don't care about your past, Alice. I want a future with you."

I held on to his gaze. "Are you OK with…everything?"

"I won't deny the *everything* took me a few days to get over," he grinned.

Hoon led me to his car. "Let's talk at home."

"Home?"

"Listen to me, my Alice from Blue Skies, we're going back to the place we make love. Tomorrow, when you wake up, there'll be no more magic seeds. We'll eat together and sleep together. Once in a while, we'll probably fight, but no matter what, we'll take our one shot *together* and see it to the end," he opened the car door for me.

The gateway droplets swelled and swirled till I could no longer see the lights I had left on at the house. Hoon knew in one lifetime what it took me two to learn: The ordinary days lived together, that's *sarang eui gijeok*.